Rescue in Poverty Gulch

Rescue in Poverty Gulch

Nancy Oswald

Filter Press, LLC
Palmer Lake, Colorado

ISBN: 978-0-86541-109-8 (Softcover)

ISBN: 978-0-86541-137-1 (Hardcover)

LCCN: 2011938306

Cover art by James P. Stroud. Copyright © 2011 James P. Stroud.

Printed in the United States of America

Manufactured by Thomson-Shore, Dexter, MI (USA); RMA577MS832, October 2011

To Mom and Dad

For fostering a love of animals and a sense of
adventure, and for letting me keep tadpoles in
the basement, a box turtle in my bedroom,
and snakes in the window well.

One

Ruby knew Maude's moods like she knew the insides of her wool stockings. The stockings right now were hot and prickly, which was just about the way her donkey was feeling—and Ruby, too, for that matter.

"She's loaded too heavy," Ruby said. Maude's back was piled high with a tent, food, clothes, Pa's books, and a supply of candleholders. She and Pa traveled around Colorado selling the candleholders to miners to use in the silver and gold mines. But this time, Pa had gotten carried away with the candleholder making. The load made Maude look like a lopsided mountain on four shaggy legs.

"Ruby, you've got to stop worrying about Maude," Pa said. "She's strong as a moosequatch." He looped the ropes around the load and cinched them tight.

"She's a grown-up donkey now."

Ruby laughed. Pa called anything big and scary a moosequatch. Then Ruby thought about Maude's age, eleven years old, same as hers. In fact, while Maude was being birthed in the barn, Ruby sucked her first breath and nearly blew the roof off the house with her wailing. That's how Pa told it, anyway.

Ruby stroked Maude's neck and spoke to her in a calming way. "We've only got about ten more miles to Cripple Creek," she told her. "Pa'll buy you ice cream when we get there."

Maude nickered when she heard "ice cream." Ruby hoped that would encourage her enough to make it up the steep, narrow road they were about to travel. Ruby didn't think Maude was afraid of heights, but the way the toll keeper told it, Shelf Road had plenty of hazards. "More than one stagecoach has plunged down into the ravine—horses, passengers, and all."

Pa tugged on the knots and took hold of Maude's lead rope. "Once we sell these candleholders," he said as they started out again, "we can travel up north. I'll show you the place you were born."

Ruby had heard Pa say this before, but every time they left town, they kept right on traveling to someplace new. Ruby supposed Pa didn't want to think about it. When Mama got sick with diphtheria, their lives changed. The very next day after she was buried, Pa packed up, locked up, closed the door to the house and, as far as Ruby knew, never looked back.

This suited Ruby just fine. She loved the rambling life just as much as Pa did. If they stayed anywhere longer than a week, Ruby's feet got twitchy. She couldn't wait to see what was over the next mountain or around the next bend, and she couldn't imagine life without golden sunsets and fresh tracks in the snow after a winter storm. Ruby figured she'd seen more of Colorado than just about any girl her age, and she had the worn-out boots to prove it.

Pa stopped for a minute to loop the lead rope around Maude's neck. Once they got going, Maude followed along without being coaxed. She rarely strayed. And for certain, she wouldn't stray today. There was only one way to get lost, and that was off the edge of the road and down over the cliff.

They started out again, climbing from the valley floor where they'd camped. "If we go up north, will I get to see my Granny and Grandpa Oliver?" Ruby asked as the road grew steeper and narrower.

"S'pose so," Pa said. "But they probably wouldn't recognize you."

"What did you tell them about me the last time you wrote?"

"I told them you're turning into the finest rattlesnake wrestler west of the Mississippi River."

Ruby grinned. She'd read Granny Oliver's last letter. "You need to settle down and find that girl a proper mother before she turns into a wild animal and makes her home in a badger hole. And she needs schooling."

Ruby didn't see what all the fuss was about. Pa had already taught her everything she needed to know. She could imitate the sounds of an owl and a meadowlark, name flowers and trees, spot wild animal tracks, and read the stars in the event someone was attacked by a moosequatch in the middle of the night and she had to go for help. Ruby even knew how to read and work with numbers, but she always hoped Pa would forget about the reading and arithmetic. He never did.

"Is the barn still there?" Ruby asked. It's the one thing she remembered clearly. When mama got ill, Pa made her a bed in the straw to keep her away from the bad air in the house. Maude liked that straw pretty well, too. She nudged Ruby out of the way, claiming half of the straw for herself. Ruby remembered how she used Maude's soft belly as a pillow.

"Still there," Pa said. "And the house, too, I reckon."

The narrow road made an abrupt turn to the left, and Ruby glanced behind them. She was surprised at how far they'd climbed. Below them, at the bottom of a narrowing canyon, Four Mile Creek disappeared and reappeared under a covering of brush. Rock outcroppings towered above the canyon walls, and the road snaked in and out and around the rocks in a maze of curves and bends.

On the inside of one of these bends, Maude slowed down and laid her ears back. "Pa," Ruby said, "Maude's getting tetchy. We'd better stop and give her a rest."

Pa took a hold of Maude's lead rope to keep her moving. "We can't rest every time Maude gets it in her mind she's overworked. Besides, I don't want to stop here on this shelf. There's no telling what might be coming around the next turn."

Ruby sighed and dropped back to walk next to Maude. She gave her a sympathetic pat on the neck. "Ice cream," Ruby said. "With a peppermint on top." Maude didn't even turn an ear to listen. Ruby couldn't remember the last time Maude was this cranky. "Pa?" Ruby tried again to convince him it was best to pamper Maude a little.

Shelf Road dipped inside, hugging the canyon wall, then curved out again to a narrow part of the road that seemed to hang in thin air above a steep drop. As they reached the curve, Maude balked and braced her legs. Pa turned and gripped Maude's lead rope with both hands and heaved. Maude pulled back the other way, edging inch by inch closer to the drop-off.

Screaming, Ruby lunged for Maude's halter to help Pa pull. Maude yielded, took two steps forward, and plunked down, packs and all, in the middle of the road. Pa cursed. "Dad gummit, Maude. You picked one fine place to have a temper tantrum." He threw the lead rope on the ground.

Ruby gasped for air, her heart pounding. She peered over the road's edge, trying not to imagine what might have happened if Maude hadn't changed her mind. "We should have let her have her a break." Ruby said.

Pa cursed again. "Well, maybe I should have fixed her up with a hotel room down in Cañon City so she was good and rested up to do a little work." He threw his hat on the ground and stomped. "And paid for a hot bath, so she could soak her hooves. Maybe shampoo her tail."

Ruby knew better than to argue with Pa when he was this upset. She shifted her eyes back and forth between Pa and Maude, trying to decide which of them was more worked up.

Pa grabbed the lead rope again. "Darn you, Maude." He turned to Ruby. "You try. She'll listen to you."

"Come on, Maudie." Ruby tugged on the rope and pleaded in her sweetest voice. "I'll make sure you get two peppermints on your ice cream."

Maude didn't budge.

"What now?" A thunder and rumbling sound shook the road. Pa grabbed Ruby and yanked her out of the road. Together, they hugged the canyon wall.

"Whoa, whoa!" The driver of the Cripple Creek stagecoach hollered. "Whoa!" The horses halted in a blow of dust, and stamped the ground, nose to nose with Maude.

"What's that donkey doing in the middle of the road?" the driver shouted. He threw the lines to the man in the shotgun seat and jumped down. He stormed toward Pa, clenching and unclenching his fists. His face grew redder with each step.

Pa didn't get a chance to answer. The driver tramped over to Maude and studied the donkey as if she were a large boulder that needed to be rolled out of the way, preferably over the side of the cliff.

One by one, the passengers unloaded. The men stretched and peered into the ravine below. A lady in a large feathery hat leaned out the coach. She lifted her skirts, stepped down, and glided over to Maude. "Isn't this just the most adorrrrrable donkey?" She turned to a woman who had followed her off the stage.

The second lady stroked Maude's white and grayish-brown nose. "Charming. Sweet as pie."

Maude toggled her ears and turned to look at her admirers, lifting her head as if she were the queen of the canyon overlook.

Exasperated, Ruby moaned. The ladies pumped up their parasols and strolled along the canyon rim as if the delay were nothing more than another social event arranged for their pleasure. Meanwhile, the conversation between Pa and the driver wasn't going so well. "That donkey has to move," the driver ordered. "I'm already behind schedule."

"Then you move her," Pa snapped.

Unhappy about the loss of attention, Maude began to bray loudly. At the same time, another voice boomed up the road behind them. "Trullee, trullee, will you be mine, sweee-eeeet sunshine? There's no better place than down ... underground ... in the Cripple Creek town."

Ruby held her hands over her ears. The song droned off-key and slurred, sounding like an animal about to die. She barely recognized it as singing.

Maude twirled one ear toward the sound, then started braying again. A chorus of donkey brays answered, echoing Maude's hello. A moment later, the singer came into sight, riding a large gray horse. A string of six donkeys clip-clopped along behind him.

When he reached the roadblock, the broad-chested man stopped and pulled a flask from his saddlebag. He uncapped it and took a swig, wetting his cracked lips. "A man sure gets thirsty on the trail." He leaned over in his saddle, offering a drink to the stagecoach driver and then to Pa.

The coach driver stomped away without so much as a nod.

Pa shook his head. "I don't drink."

"Then how about you, Little Missy?" He held out the flask toward Ruby.

Little Missy! Ruby took a strong disliking to the man. His black mustache was waxed and turned up in tight twists, and somewhere, in the shadow of his black hat, Ruby imagined two snakelike eyes. She glowered at him, and the reflection from the handle of his gun glared back at her.

The man took another swig. "Looks like you've got a donkey problem."

A donkey problem! Ruby bristled, and Maude snorted—a sound she saved for people she didn't like.

The man capped his flask. "Doesn't look like she's fixin' to go anywhere soon," he said. "I can haul some of your belongings up the mountain— lighten her load—for a price."

Pa's neck muscles tensed. He frowned.

"Of course, you could stash your things in the rocks," the man added. "But they might not be here when you come back. Lots a thieves around." He chuckled.

"How much will it cost me?" Pa asked.

"Ten would probably do it."

Pa's jaw popped back and forth like a tiny door

opening and closing. He glanced at Maude one more time and slowly dug into his pocket, and counted out the bills. Ruby stared in disbelief.

"Hawker." The man slid off the saddle and took the money. "Jake Hawker."

"Tom Oliver," Pa said in a not-very-friendly way. He started to unload Maude, putting the heavy iron candleholders in one pile and their day-to-day necessities in another. He added the tent and camping gear to the pile for Hawker to haul to Cripple Creek.

"What about your books?" Ruby asked. She'd never known Pa to go anywhere without his books. Pa hesitated, then added them to the "necessity" pile.

"For another ten, I could haul it all," Hawker said, tying the bundles of candleholders onto his lead donkey's back.

Pa scowled. "No, just tell me where I can pick up my property."

"If I get there ahead of you, and it looks like I will," Hawker looked at Maude and back at Pa, "I'll leave the bundle at the El Paso Livery on Bennett Avenue and First." He uncapped the flask, took another long draw, and staggered back to his horse.

With the passengers' help, the stagecoach driver inched his team backward to where the road was a little wider. There was just enough room for Hawker to weave his donkey caravan around Maude and past the stage. As he headed up the trail again, he crooned his drunken song. Long after he was out of sight, they could still hear the sour notes echoing off the canyon walls.

"Pa!" Ruby blurted as the last notes faded. "That man charged more money than you make in a week!"

Pa picked up his hat, dusted it, and jammed it on his head. "Didn't seem like we had much choice."

"You goin' to move now?" The stagecoach driver hollered from his seat.

Ruby coaxed Maude up and helped Pa tie their remaining belongings to the packsaddle. Maude consented to being led out of the way, and they watched the coach go, a hanky waving from one of the windows. Playfully, Maude nudged Ruby. Ruby scratched Maude above her tail, relieved that she'd returned to her cheerful self.

Pa was a different story. "At this rate, we'll be lucky to get to Cripple Creek before midnight." He wiped sweat from his brow with the sleeve of his shirt. "If we have any more of Maude's shenanigans..."

Before he could finish his threat, they heard a loud crash. "Whoa! Whoa!" Ruby turned to see the left rear wheel of the stagecoach slip into a washout at the edge of the road. The coach rocked forward and backward then jiggled to a halt. Ruby covered Maude's ears at the string of curses that streamed from the stagecoach driver. Pa grumbled and started toward the tipping rig. "Can't just leave them stranded," he said as he passed Ruby.

Two

The passengers climbed out again. This time, the ladies were not so cheerful. The men removed their coats and gathered around the rear of the coach to lift and push. Pa collected flat stones, and each time the men heaved, he layered one under the wheel to prop it up. Inch by inch, the stagecoach rose until the back wheel was level with the road, balanced on the wobbly rocks.

Ruby held her breath as the driver clucked to the horses and eased the coach forward onto solid ground. He hollered and snapped the lines. The last passenger barely had time to jump in and swing the door closed before the coach started rolling again. A copy of the *Cripple Creek Times* tumbled out of the stagecoach and landed in the dust. Ruby picked it up and studied the date. April 1, 1896. "Pa," Ruby said, "it's April Fools' Day!"

"It figures," Pa said, looking up at the sky to judge the time. "And we'll be fools if we have to camp out tonight without our tent."

* * *

The sun was sinking behind a cone-shaped mountain to the west when they reached the outskirts of Cripple Creek. Maude's ears perked and swiveled left and right at all the new sounds and smells. When they reached Bennett Avenue, Ruby's attention mirrored Maude's. Her eyes darted in all directions as men rolled barrels of beer into gambling halls, vendors hawked their goods, and a blind preacher stood on a corner and read from an upside-down Bible.

While Pa went into the livery, Ruby examined everyone along the street. People dressed every which way, from torn pants and patched jackets to three-piece suits. Men wore miner's hats, top hats, derbies, and boaters. Women with parasols strolled the boardwalk in glittery gowns, wrapped in light shawls to keep out the cool mountain air. Other women wore day dresses or more practical frocks for work or casual outings.

Beyond the bustling streets, the snowcapped peak that Pa had called Pikes Peak towered above the town. The lower hills were dotted with head frames and ore houses marking the places where gold was brought to the surface and processed. Smoke belched from brick chimneys, and the rattle of mining machinery clattered from the hillside, making Ruby want to cover her ears. She wondered if the town ever slept.

Pa was taking a long time. Ruby pulled Maude out of the way and leaned against the side of the livery to wait. A woman wearing a feathered hat swayed toward them, the hat feathers bobbing back and forth and up and down. Ruby tried to decide what birds they had come from. She ran through a list of yellow birds she knew: prairie warbler, Western meadowlark, goldfinch, yellow-headed blackbird … and there was a mix of something blue … and something speckled …

The birds swerved unexpectedly and flew from Ruby's mind. The woman perched on the seat of a type of bicycle Ruby had never seen before. She wore an outfit that was hard to describe. It wasn't really a dress, but two puffy skirts. Each skirt gathered below one of her knees, barely touching the shiny black boots that pumped the pedals.

Pa picked this moment to storm out of the livery into the street. He yowled, "If I ever see that Jake Hawker again, I'm going to stuff him into his whiskey flask and put a cork in it."

Ruby shrieked as Pa stepped into the path of the

bicycle. The front wheel of the contraption wrenched sideways, and the woman flew over the handlebars, toppling Pa and taking him down with her. Ruby gaped at the tangle of arms and legs and hats and boots thrashing on the ground at her feet.

The woman stood first, brushing the skirts of her riding clothes and tucking stray strands of black hair underneath her feathered hat, which had miraculously stayed on her head. She pulled her shoulders back, drew in her chin, and tightened her lips into a line that nearly disappeared into her flushed cheeks.

Pa stammered. "I'm sorry ma'am. I didn't see you." He picked up the bicycle.

"I suggest you look more carefully next time." The woman's voice sounded as rigid as the handlebars of her bicycle.

In a precise and methodical manner, she checked for damage, wheel to wheel, starting at the back and working forward. "There's no impairment that I can see." She lifted one hand to her face. "Oh my." She bent over like a long-legged bird and frantically groped at the ground around her feet.

"Is this what you're looking for?" Ruby held out a pair of spectacles that had landed in the dirt.

"Yes, thank you." She straightened the bent ear wires and placed them on her nose. They tipped sideways, giving her a slightly lopsided look. Then, as if realizing she could see clearly again, the woman frowned, studying Ruby from the tip of her head down to her scuffed and dirty boots.

"Young lady," she said sternly. "Why haven't I seen you in school?"

"School?" Ruby nearly choked on the word. "I don't go to school, and I don't plan to start anytime soon."

The woman jolted upright, and the spectacles tilted a little more.

"We just got into town," Pa explained. He removed his hat and introduced himself. "Tom Oliver, and this is my daughter, Ruby."

Pa nudged Ruby and waited. "Pleased to meet you." She curtsied. Ruby wished Pa wouldn't encourage her to lie.

"I'm Miss Sternum, the school principal." The woman nodded abruptly. "How long do you plan to stay?"

"Might be longer than we thought," Pa said.

"Very well," Miss Sternum said. "I'll expect to see Ruby at school as soon as you are settled." Without another word, she mounted her bicycle and pedaled away, the feathers on her hat slicing the horizon as she rode.

"Pa," Ruby said as Miss Sternum disappeared, "we won't be here long enough for me to go to school, will we?"

"That's what I was trying to tell you when I got tangled up with that bicycle. We don't have a single candleholder to sell. That scoundrel, Jake Hawker, stole everything he loaded on that donkey."

"Everything?" Ruby thought about their tent and camping gear.

"Gone," Pa said. He squeezed his hat angrily. "And if I ever see that Hawker again …"

Ruby knew Pa always had a little money saved up for what he called rough times. "Can't we make some more candleholders and move on?"

Pa sighed and loosened his grip on his hat. He placed it on his head. "'The web of our life is of a mingled yarn, good and ill together.' Shakespeare."

There were times Ruby wished Pa hadn't had so much book learning. "Can't you just say it out plain?"

"In spite of our misfortune, I've been offered a job in the livery. We've managed to find good luck in the middle of the bad."

Luck? Once, Ruby hit a rabbit with her slingshot on the first try. That was *her* idea of luck.

"And there was a fellow in there told me about a cabin we could rent if we hurry. Places up here don't last long."

Ruby thought about this sudden turn of events. The day had started out like any other—a cool morning breeze, the smell of coffee on the campfire.

Now Pa had a job and wanted to rent a cabin. She took a deep breath. *Had Pa lost his mind?* He wouldn't like living under a roof any more than she would. Ruby glanced down the street, not wanting to look at him. About half a block away, she spotted Maude, ambling along, her lead rope dragging. Maude looked as if she were one of the evening walkers, out for a breath of fresh air.

"Pa!" Ruby pointed. She dashed after Maude with Pa at her heels. She ran east on Bennett past Slusher's Grocery and zigzagged around groups of men talking and unloading crates of supplies from wagons. Breathlessly, she caught up to Maude in front of a tall plate glass window with a sign above it that read Palace Drug. Maude looked through the glass into the store. It took Ruby a minute to make out the words "Ice Cream" painted in large letters on the face of the glass, but Maude seemed to have read them from far down the street.

Maude brayed loudly as Pa dug into his pocket for change. "That darn Hawker," Pa grumbled and handed the money to Ruby. "Three penny licks are all I can afford. After I get my first pay, we'll come back for more."

Three

Two days later, the memory of the ice cream had faded. *Gone*, Ruby thought. *Melted like the summer snow from a mountain glacier.* Ice cream usually smoothed over a lot of things, but it would take a serving the size of Pikes Peak for Ruby to forgive Pa for this. Pa had decided to settle down.

"He's never wanted to stay in one place before," Ruby confided in Maude. They stood outside a small rented cabin. "Living inside is worse than jail."

Maude nuzzled Ruby. "At least you understand." Ruby patted Maude's head then combed her sides with a stiff bristled brush. Maude made a donkey murmur, and Ruby wondered if Pa would let her camp outside with Maude instead of sleeping inside.

Ruby thought about the things Pa had bought for the cabin: new pots and pans, a fancy saltcellar, and a red-and-white-checkered cloth to cover the small wooden table. *Fussy stuff for a one-room shack,* Ruby thought. Her blood boiled every time she thought about the trouble that Hawker man had caused. If Hawker hadn't stolen their candleholders, they'd have sold most of them by now and be on their way out of town, sleeping under the stars—not fancying up some cabin.

"And Pa's got it in his mind that I should go to school." Ruby choked on the word *school.* Today, in just a few minutes, life would be over for Ruby May Oliver.

"You ready?" Ruby turned at his words. She hadn't heard the cabin door open and close. Pa had trimmed his mustache and put on a clean shirt. Something sweet floated around him.

"What's that smell?" She didn't wait for an answer. "It's shaving stuff, isn't it?"

Pa changed the subject. "You can tie Maude up to the shed. She'll be fine until you come home."

Ruby folded her arms across her chest. "I'm not going to school without Maude." She wanted to tell Pa she wasn't going at all, but she'd already tried that and Pa didn't like that idea much.

"If you don't fold in that lower lip, a chicken is going to use it for a roost."

Ruby tucked in her lip but continued to frown. She wasn't about to let him tease her out of a sour mood.

"School's no place for a donkey," Pa said. "What's Maude going to do all day?"

"She needs to work on her numbers," Ruby said stubbornly.

Pa laughed and tugged on Ruby's long brown braid. "Maybe that Jake Hawker did us a favor by heisting our gear. I think your ma would like it if you had some real schooling."

Ma! Pa hardly ever mentioned Ma unless he was set on getting Ruby to do something she didn't want to do. It was the last card in his deck. "Ma wouldn't want me separated from Maude. We've never been apart." Ruby played her ace.

Pa relented. "I don't suppose it would do any harm if Maude walked with us," he sighed. "I'll bring her back here before I head over to the livery."

Ruby relaxed a little. They started west on El Paso Avenue, passing rows of tents and frame shacks, then turned up South Fourth Street. At Irene Street they turned west, crossing the turnaround tracks for the Florence and Cripple Creek Railroad, then turned back to the north until they reached Warren Avenue. It was a straight shot west from there to the school at First Street and Warren.

Downtown Cripple Creek wasn't far from where they turned. Ruby heard a loud whistle from a train arriving on the Midland line. Smoke belched into the air from its engine as it squealed down the grade. She'd never get used to the noise. Never! Ruby slowed and walked behind Pa. She was so busy feeling sorry for herself, she didn't notice the two boys behind her.

"That donkey has freckles," a voice said.

"Or maybe it's just mud," a second voice said.

Ruby turned to look as the boys got closer to Maude. The boys were half her size, and one of them wore a red cap tipped down over his right ear. The other wore bibbed overalls two sizes too big.

"Never seen a donkey with markings like this one." The red-capped boy pointed to a few spots on Maude's otherwise white belly. "What's her name?"

"Maude," Ruby said impatiently.

"My name's Josef, and my brother, here, is Franz."

Ruby ignored the boys. She quick-stepped to catch up with Pa, but a jerk on Maude's lead rope pulled her backward. She looked back and saw Maude taking a big bite from a carrot Franz held out to her.

"Better not let Ma find out you're feeding your lunch to a donkey," Josef said. "Ain't much left in the root cellar."

Maude chomped the second half of the carrot and nudged the boy's shoulder for more. "Can't give you my bread," Franz said, tucking his lunch back inside the bib of his overalls. "There wouldn't be nothin' left for me."

Josef spoke to Ruby. "This here's a fine donkey. Where you taking her?"

"To school," Ruby said, yanking on Maude's rope to get her going again.

The boys laughed and jogged alongside. "There ain't gonna be a desk big enough for her."

Ruby huffed and walked more quickly, trying to catch up with Pa.

"Don't be mad," Franz said, scampering to catch up. "We like donkeys, but most donkeys around here are work animals. They don't go to school."

"This donkey works. He works for us," Ruby said. She glanced over at Pa to make sure he heard. "Me and my pa got a business selling candleholders."

"How come you're not selling them?"

Ruby pictured their candleholder bundles tipping and swaying up the hill behind Jake Hawker and decided the story would take too long to tell. It wasn't any of their business, anyway. As the school came into view, the boys skipped past, leaving Ruby one last chance to convince Pa that formal education was a waste of time.

"I'm not going in," Ruby said as they approached the school steps.

Pa frowned. "Now Ruby, we've already talked this through."

"But ..."

"Mr. Oliver, I see you've come to enroll your daughter." A woman came down the front steps of the two-story brick building. It took Ruby a minute to recognize Miss Sternum. She wore a black skirt with a high-collared, stiffly starched white blouse. There were no stray hairs, and her glasses had been straightened, making her look even sterner than she had outside of the livery.

"I'm afraid she's a little reluctant," Pa said.

Miss Sternum pursed her lips. "How much schooling did you say she's had?"

Pa started to explain when Ruby blurted, "I can read and do numbers. I figure that's about all the schooling I need."

Miss Sternum frowned at Ruby. "Miss Oliver, do you always interrupt your elders when they are speaking?"

Ruby plowed right on. "And I can prove it to you."

"Well," Miss Sternum said with an edge to her voice. "That's exactly what we will ask you to do." She turned a heel and started up the steps, leaving no doubt that Ruby was to follow.

"Pa?" Ruby gave him one last pleading look.

He folded his arms across his chest, and with a severe look of his own, nodded his head toward the double doors at the top of the steps. *I've been betrayed,* Ruby thought, as she pounded up the steps and entered the halls of doom. The last thing she heard before the doors closed behind her was Maude's loud bray as Pa led her away.

Four

Ruby fidgeted. The desk wrapped around her like a stiff harness. It hadn't taken her long to prove to Miss Sternum that she knew a thing or two about book learning. Now she wasn't sure if she should have. She'd been moved to a room with the older students and a teacher named Miss Logan. Miss Logan was as clean and starched as Miss Sternum, and Ruby began to wonder if frowning was part of a teacher's job.

Ruby's desk was behind a girl whose blonde hair was braided and pinned to the back of her head, reminding Ruby of a coiled snake. Agnes Gribbell, Ruby decided, was the teacher's pet. Her arm shot up as if Miss Logan were a puppeteer and had a string tied to it.

"Five times eight?" Miss Logan called out multiplication problems for practice.

Agnes's hand flew up, but before Miss Logan called on her, Ruby blurted, "Forty."

Miss Logan shot Ruby an angry look. "Four times six?"

"Twenty-four," Ruby shouted, feeling smug.

A patch of color appeared above Miss Logan's starched collar. It crept up to her ears, and spread like beet juice on her cheeks. She stopped the lesson and spoke firmly. "Miss Oliver, you have proven very well that you understand the lessons, but you do not understand how to raise your hand."

Ruby scanned the room. Everyone sat stiff-backed, staring straight ahead. Slowly, she lifted her hand, showing that she knew how. A titter started somewhere behind her and spread like the measles. Soon, the entire class was laughing.

Miss Logan picked up the ruler from the top of her desk and slapped it in the palm of her hand as she paced. "Miss Oliver," she began again, "I am quite sure the schools you have attended in the past did not tolerate this kind of behavior."

Ruby thought back over the conversations she'd had with Miss Sternum. She'd only told Miss Sternum that she knew how to read and do numbers. This morning, Pa never got a chance to explain. Ruby inched her hand up again. "I've never been to school, ma'am."

Lester Ward, a chunky boy who slumped in a desk near the window, muttered, "I wish I'd never been to school." The students started to laugh again, then stopped abruptly when their teacher slapped the ruler on her desk.

"We do not tolerate fibs. I'm quite certain you learned to read somewhere." Miss Logan hissed like Pa's coffee when it boiled over into the fire.

Ruby never fibbed. *Almost never,* she corrected herself. She certainly would never fib about where she learned to read. Ruby decided she wouldn't say anything at all. Even if she knew the answer, she would sit quietly and watch. Pa had taught her that about nature. You had to be quiet and look closely to understand animals and their behaviors.

Ruby studied two boys on the window side of the room. The big one, Lester Ward, sat next to a skinny boy, who spat tobacco into a cup that he hid when Miss Logan looked his way. When Miss Logan called on him, Ruby learned that his name was Roy O'Rourke. Once he almost got caught spitting. Ruby watched as his face turned a pale green after he swallowed the tobacco juice.

When Ruby tired of watching Roy O'Rourke chew and spit, she worked on getting comfortable in the hard wooden seat. She slumped down, leaned sideways and forward, wiggled, and balanced her chin on her elbows. Agnes turned around and frowned.

Ruby frowned back, then slouched and settled into a daydream about the Black Canyon of the Gunnison, wild whitecapped rapids bouncing between the cliffs, hawks soaring, and the sweet smell of pine. She was helping Pa build a campfire when Lester Ward stood up and pressed his face against the window.

"Miss Logan, there's a donkey out there trying to ride on our teeter-totter."

Students flew from their desks to the window. Ruby wiggled to the front for a clear view. Maude had one hoof perched on the end of a thick wooden board that was balanced on a stout log. With her frayed rope dangling, she carefully took a step, then walked up the timber until her front hooves were near the tipping point.

Ruby gaped, thinking about all the hours she and Pa had spent teaching Maude to cross narrow planked bridges. Maude took another step and the board shifted ever so slightly, leaving Maude balanced on the top.

"Whose donkey is it?" someone asked.

"It's hers," a short girl with a ponytail pointed at Ruby. "I seen her walking with it this morning."

"She looks like one of them circus animals, balancing on a ball," Lester said.

"Those. One of *those* circus animals." Miss Logan started to direct the class back to their desks. Maude took another step. The board tipped, and she trotted down, kicking at the plank with her back legs as it hit the ground and bounced back up.

The children laughed, and even Miss Logan smiled. "Stupid donkey," the boy called Roy said.

Ruby felt a prickle of irritation. As the students returned to their seats, Ruby followed Roy to his desk and stood over him with her hands on her hips. "That donkey is not stupid." She narrowed her eyes, ready to tell Roy a thing or two. The room fell silent.

Just when she thought she might need to impress Roy with her strength, someone pointed to the window. "There she goes again." Maude had circled back around to the other side and was attempting to make another crossing on the teeter-totter.

"Miss Oliver," Miss Logan's voice rose in volume, "please go outside and take care of that animal."

Ruby hurried outside. She took hold of Maude's frayed rope and led her to a tree at the edge of the playground. "I don't think Miss Logan likes you." She looped what remained of Maude's rope around a low branch and tied it tightly. Maude nickered and nudged Ruby's forearm. "I'll come see you when it's dinnertime. That is, if we ever get to eat."

Ruby slid back into her desk, trying to get comfortable all over again. Miss Logan stood next to an easel with a large map on it, explaining the geography of the United States. Ruby perked up. The state of Colorado, which Ruby knew to be her whole world, was only a small rectangle surrounded by other shapes with slants and squiggly lines.

Miss Logan swept her hand across the map. "Who in this class can name the states?" She tapped on the map again.

Still trying to grasp the idea, Ruby leaned forward. *Why hadn't Pa told her about all those other states?* She only knew about New Mexico because they had crossed the border once. Even then, Ruby hadn't noticed anything different about it. She couldn't wait to tell Pa about this. He'd surely want to pack up and set off to traveling again.

Interested now, Ruby listened as her classmates recited the names of the states surrounding Colorado or nearby. Agnes was the last to answer, and she recited a list of states longer than the Arkansas River—which Ruby now knew passed through a state by the name of Kansas and then joined an even bigger river named the Mississippi. Miss Logan smiled at Agnes, and then using a long slender stick, she pointed out the state capitals.

About the time Miss Logan started talking about all the fish and something called natural resources, Ruby drifted off again, this time daydreaming about the trout Pa had caught in the Purgatory River down near Durango. He had rolled the trout in cornmeal and fried it up over the fire. Ruby's stomach started to grumble. Now her mind wandered to what Pa had put in that lard bucket he'd handed to her before he left.

Ruby moved like lightning when the class was dismissed for the noon break. She zigzagged around a marble game and made a beeline to the other side of the playground where Maude stood. "You wouldn't believe what it's like in there." Ruby stroked one of Maude's ears. "The windows are shut up so tight, not even an ant can crawl through."

Settling herself near Maude, Ruby stretched out her cramped legs, arranged her dress, and sank her teeth into the jam and bread Pa had packed. After eating, she lay back on the ground, soaking up the sunshine and inhaling the fresh mountain air. She closed her eyes, daydreaming about life on the trail. Her good humor had returned.

Ruby's daydreams came to a sudden halt when she heard Maude bray—the kind of bray that she recognized as a call of distress. Ruby sat up abruptly. Maude had wandered to the middle of the playground and was surrounded by a small group of children. "Yee hah!" Ruby heard a shout.

Grabbing her lunch bucket, Ruby leapt up and ran over. Roy O'Rourke sat on top of Maude, kicking her hard in the sides trying to get her to buck like a rodeo bronco. Ruby elbowed her way to the front of the small crowd and yanked Roy by the arm. He tumbled off Maude and hit the ground, coming up swinging. Ruby ducked, throwing Roy off balance. He stumbled forward, grabbing the hem of her dress. He pulled her down. Ooomf! Ruby swung at empty air.

Maude brayed louder, and Ruby heard someone holler, "Fight! Fight!" Ruby dropped her lunch pail and grabbed Roy's legs, bringing him down. His sharp elbow clipped her right eye as he fell, and he landed nose first. *Serves him right!* She was reaching for her lunch pail to whack Roy over the head when a hand from above grabbed the collar of her dress and lifted her to her feet.

Ruby couldn't see who was doing the pulling, but from the look on Roy's face as he scrambled to attention it had to be either a grizzly bear or a moosequatch. By now it seemed as though every student in the school had gathered around. Maude had skeedaddled and was nowhere to be seen.

"Young lady!" Ruby knew that voice. "This type of behavior is not appropriate at the Warren Avenue School." As the grip loosened, Ruby turned to see Miss Sternum, towering above her. Her face looked as if she'd just eaten the sourest lemon in the barrel at Slusher's Grocery.

"I'm sorry Miss Sternum," Roy said. "She threw

me on the ground. I didn't have a choice." Blood dripped from his nose.

"Young man, in this world we *always* have a choice."

Roy wiped the blood from his upper lip and hung his head. If he were a dog, Ruby thought, his tail would be tucked in so far it would wrap under his belly and come up under his chin.

"And what do you have to say for yourself, Miss Oliver?" Miss Sternum asked.

Ruby didn't have anything to say for herself, but she sure wanted to tell Roy a thing or two. She folded her arms across her chest and glared straight into his eyes, trying to sizzle him with her gaze.

"Very well, then," Miss Sternum said. "I'll see you in my office." She turned to Miss Logan who had joined the group. "Please deliver the usual punishment for fighting to Mr. O'Rourke. I'll tend to Miss Oliver."

Ruby felt her eye swelling as she followed Miss Sternum up the front steps of the school. This was her second trip to the principal's office today. The first time was to check Ruby's readin' and 'rithmetic skills. Miss Sternum had offered her a chair then. Something about this visit did not seem as friendly. Ruby shifted from foot to foot as Miss Sternum took a seat behind her polished hardwood desk.

Miss Sternum rested her chin on her folded

hands and leaned forward, studying Ruby through her spectacles. The silence seemed to last for hours. "This is *not* a very auspicious beginning."

Auspicious. Ruby didn't think she'd ever heard Pa use that word. If something was *not* auspicious, it couldn't be good. She started to worry.

"Your mother," Miss Sternum asked, "will she be joining you here in Cripple Creek at a later date?"

"I don't reckon," Ruby said.

Miss Sternum cleared her throat and tried again. "You and your father live alone?"

"No, ma'am. We've got Maude."

"Maude? Is she a relative?"

Ruby had to think about that for a moment. "I suppose she is."

"And she lives with you?" Miss Sternum seemed to be trying to put the pieces of the puzzle together.

Ruby smiled and nodded.

"Very well. Perhaps Maude will be some help with your school adjustment." Miss Sternum took paper from the drawer of her desk, reached for a fountain pen, and began to write. She wrote what looked to Ruby like the date, then stopped. "Does Maude have a last name?"

"Oliver," Ruby said without hesitation.

Miss Sternum drummed her fingers on the desk and studied Ruby again. "Maude is your aunt?"

"No ma'am."

"A cousin, then?"

Ruby shook her head no.

Impatiently, Miss Sternum asked. "Am I clear that you all have the same residence?"

"Residence?" Ruby thought it probably meant the cabin, but she wasn't sure.

"You all live under the same roof?" Miss Sternum urged.

Ruby shook her head, no. "Since we got the cabin, Pa makes Maude sleep outside."

Miss Sternum sighed in exasperation. She looked down at her paper where a blob of ink had pooled underneath the tip of her pen. Crumpling the letter into a ball, she tossed it into the wastebasket. She took out a clean sheet and started again.

Ruby cleared her throat. "If you're fixin' to write Maude, she can't read."

Miss Sternum wrinkled her brow. "Besides," Ruby said, "it'd be a lot easier if you just went outside and talked to her."

"Who?" Miss Sternum appeared confused.

"Maude," Ruby said. "She's the reason I had to fight Roy. And I'll fight him again if he doesn't treat her with a little more respect."

Maude chose this moment to walk by the front of the school in plain view of Miss Sternum's office window.

"It seems I need to have a conversation with

Miss … Mrs …" Miss Sternum paused. "With this relative of yours."

"You can," Ruby said, pointing out the window. "She's right outside."

Miss Sternum stood up and turned slowly around to the window. Her shoulders lifted and dropped and lifted again as she inhaled and exhaled deeply. There was a long moment before she spoke. "*That* … is Maude?"

"Yes, ma'am," Ruby said.

Miss Sternum plunked back down into her chair, picked up her fountain pen, and without looking up, began to write. When she finished, she folded the letter, sealed it, and held it out to Ruby. "Please see that your father gets this. Tonight."

Five

Ruby didn't figure it would do any good to open the letter and try to read it. She had watched Miss Sternum use the swirly-curly writing that Pa never used. His handwriting was firm and used short strokes. When Ruby got home, she placed the letter on Pa's cot, then paced around the cabin, finally deciding it would be in her best interest to tidy up and maybe get some supper going before Pa came home.

Ruby glanced around. They hadn't lived in the cabin long enough to muss things up, so there wasn't much to do. She smoothed the new red tablecloth, swept the floor, and looked around for something to straighten. Pa's shaving mirror was hanging at a tilt from a nail on the wall next to his cot. As Ruby stopped to level it, she got a first glimpse of the damage to her face. No gashes on the left side—a little smudge of dirt—but no blood.

The right side of her face was a different matter. She patted the swollen place where Roy's elbow had struck underneath her right eye. A purplish-blue color spread from the swelling toward her nose and around to the top of her eye. Ruby decided her face didn't look much worse than her dirt-stained and torn wool dress. She found the mending kit and started on the repairs.

Pa came home smiling. "How's my ruby-red Ruby?" He threw his hat on the table and sat on the cot to take off his boots. Paper crinkled underneath him. Pa pulled out the wrinkled envelope. "What's this?" He looked over to Ruby's cot where she sat sewing. "Something from your teacher?"

"Miss Sternum," Ruby said.

Pa eyed Ruby carefully. "Were you at school today, or did you decide to run off and become a raccoon?"

Ruby plunked down her mending. She spilled out the whole story about Maude breaking her lead rope and coming to school, and how that mean and rotten Roy O'Rourke gave her a black eye, and last but not least how she ended up spending time with Miss Sternum in a room that would make a jail cell look comfortable.

Pa lifted an eyebrow at Ruby. He opened the envelope, unfolded the letter, and began to read, nodding every once in a while, adding an "uh huh" or "um." When he finished, he rifled through a packsaddle bag and pulled out a pencil. He used his pocketknife to sharpen it to a fine point, then sat down at the table. At the bottom of the letter, he wrote a few words and handed it to Ruby. "Make sure Miss Sternum gets this when you go back to school tomorrow."

"I'm going back?" Ruby pointed at her face and groaned. "But Pa ..."

"Ruby May Oliver, when did a black eye ever stop you? I remember the time you skinned both knees chasing a fox, got up, kept running, and slipped in the creek. You ended up with a goose egg on your head as big as Maude's nose."

"That was different," Ruby said. She eyed the letter, wishing she could read Miss Sternum's handwriting. Pa's scrawl was easy, but what he wrote was as hard to understand as Miss Sternum's curly writing. *Miss Sternum, I'll make sure Ruby attends and is properly attired. Regards, Mr. Tom Oliver.*

Ruby waited until Pa had left for the livery the next morning to look at the letter again. She carefully unfolded it and skimmed Miss Sternum's handwriting, picking out "Oliver" and "Ruby" and "Maude." The word "Ruby" was scattered like raindrops down the page. At the end, Ruby picked out Miss Sternum's name, but there was something in between "Miss" and "Sternum." Probably her first name.

Ruby tried to imagine a first name that fit Miss Sternum. Miss Frowny Sternum, Miss Upright Sternum, Miss Standing-Straight Sternum, Miss Rigid-and-Unbending Sternum ...

Ruby struggled once more to read the letter. She made out another name. A-G-N-E-S and then after that a word that looked like *pretty* or *patty*. Ruby folded the letter and put it inside her lunch pail. She decided she'd attend school, at least long enough to learn to write the swirly-curly way. How long could it take? A day or two, and it might come in handy someday.

Ruby headed up the hill toward Warren Avenue. The only good thing about her black eye was that Ruby had convinced Pa she needed a friend at school, and he agreed to let Maude go with her. "As long as she behaves," Pa had said, then after a pause added, "as long as you *both* behave."

★ ★ ★

Ruby didn't think much more about the letter until Friday afternoon, when she saw Pa waiting for her at the bottom of the school steps. He already had Maude in hand, and by the look on his face, he had a purpose in mind. For a moment, Ruby let herself hope that he'd decided it was time to pack up and move on. That hope faded as they started toward the center of town, and Pa announced it was time she had a new dress.

"It's only April," Ruby complained. They usually didn't buy new clothes until May or June when the weather turned hot.

"You're going to need a new dress," Pa said, "for the party tomorrow."

Party! Ruby remembered the word that looked like "pretty" and "patty" in the letter. *This was Miss Sternum's doing!* Ruby swiped at a stray hair that seemed to pop out of her long braid when she was upset.

"It's a social tea," Pa continued. "For girls in your class."

Ruby brightened a little. "Will there be cookies and tea cakes to eat?"

"Probably so," Pa said. "Your mama used to hold teas, and Granny Oliver, too."

"Was I ever at one?" Ruby wanted to know. "I mean before…"

"You were the sweetest cupcake at the party," Pa said.

Ruby supposed if it were something Mama liked to do, she would give it a try. She had a notion Maude would like it, too—especially if there were treats. She thought about teacakes all the way to the clothing store at Bennett and Third.

Inside the store, Ruby stopped and stared. She'd been in many stores on their travels, but this one topped them all. There was a forest of shoes, stockings, skirts, blouses, suits, pants, and other clothing of all styles and sizes.

"May I help you?"

Pa pushed Ruby forward a step and said, "My daughter needs a couple of new dresses," Pa said. "One for every day and a party dress suitable for a tea."

"Pa!" This was the first time he'd mentioned two dresses, and she wasn't sure at all about the fancy one.

The saleslady gently took Ruby by the arm. "I believe I can take care of this if you'd like to come back later." She winked at Pa and waved him out the front door of the store.

She inspected Ruby from head to toe. "It *does* look like you could use a new dress." The woman glanced over at the ready-made section then back again, measuring Ruby with her eyes. "A school dress," the lady spoke to herself and selected one, holding it up next to Ruby for size.

"Do you have anything like the one I'm wearing?"

The saleswoman's gaze lingered on the patched-up places on Ruby's wool jumper and spots where campfire smoke and spills had made their own pattern across the skirt. The saleslady nodded and selected another one—grayish brown—made of heavy fabric. "This looks, um, practical."

Ruby began to warm to the woman. The dress was a good choice—plain with big pockets for rocks or maybe marbles.

"And now for the party dress." The saleswoman put a finger to her chin and walked over to another rack of girls' dresses. She held one up for Ruby to see. "This style is quite popular."

Ruby puckered her brow. The dress was yellow and frilly with puffy sleeves. She couldn't imagine hauling wood in it.

The woman didn't give Ruby time to object. "And I think it will fit just perfectly. But you'll need a corset for underneath. Most of the young ladies in Cripple Creek of your age are already wearing them. It will make both dresses fit better."

A corset! Ruby knew what that was—a cinch that girls wore underneath their clothing. She thought about how Maude grunted every time Pa tightened her packsaddle, and she wanted nothing to do with wearing a corset.

The saleswoman had other ideas. By the time Pa returned, Ruby had been bound, trussed, and cinched up. She wore her new everyday dress and held the yellow one under her arm, wrapped in brown paper. She shifted uncomfortably, wanting to hurry home so she could loosen up.

As Pa paid, the salesclerk asked, "What would you like me to do with this?" She held Ruby's old dress at an arms' length, as if it were alive and might bite her.

"I'll take it." Ruby snatched it out of the saleswoman's hands.

Six

On Saturday, promptly at 2:00 p.m., Ruby made her way up Third Street. She was thinking that if it were summer, every bee within 10 miles would be landing on her puffy yellow sleeves trying to collect nectar. At the very last minute, Pa had decided to buy her some new shoes, too, so all in all, Ruby felt like a cross between a frilly curtain and a curtain rod.

"You're going to have to be on your best manners today," Ruby told Maude as they turned the corner at Eaton Avenue and started west. She was pretty sure Pa wouldn't have wanted her to bring Maude, but he wasn't around to ask. He'd gone to the livery early and planned to stay late so he could use the forge to start making candleholders.

Ruby walked two blocks and looked for a two-story house with an upper-story porch with a white railing around it. She thought it would be easy to pick out but soon discovered that Agnes's house was not the only big one. To Ruby, they all seemed like mansions.

Ruby stopped in front of a house that fit Miss Sternum's description and studied it. Four girls raced down the front steps and crowded around Maude, petting and cooing over her. A girl named Sadie scratched behind Maude's right ear. Agnes giggled and scratched behind the other one. Sandwiched between the ear-scratchers, Maude made a throaty noise. If she'd been a cat, it would have sounded like purring.

A sharp command came from the porch. "Get away from that animal! You'll get your dress dirty."

Agnes reluctantly pulled back, but the other girls kept stroking. "I wish I had a donkey like Maude," a girl named Mary said.

"Me, too." Sadie leaned in and gave Maude a hug.

Ruby shifted impatiently, wanting to get on with the party when, Eloise, the shyest of the girls, noticed her new clothes. "Did your Pa buy you a new dress?"

The girls stopped admiring Maude and started fussing over Ruby's puffy yellow sleeves.

"New shoes, too." Sadie pointed. The girls cooed over the polished kid leather and the white bows on the toes. Ruby blushed at the attention. If she hadn't been afraid that Pa would find out, she would have worn her trail boots. At least they were comfortable.

At that moment, Miss Sternum pedaled up on her bicycle. She nodded with approval when she saw Ruby. At the same time, Mrs. Gribbell called to them from the side of the house. Ruby tied Maude to a small bush in the front yard and followed the other girls to the backyard. The weather was mild, and sunlight danced off the silverware that was laid out on a long table covered with a white linen tablecloth.

A plate of cookies and a tray filled with jam tarts pulled Ruby forward like a magnet. She started to the table but noticed the other girls were waiting. Mrs. Gribbell pointed to each girl's place. Ruby sat between Miss Sternum and Mary, across from Agnes and Eloise. Mrs. Gribbell took her place at the head of the table.

Ruby watched carefully. She sipped cautiously when the tea was poured, trying not to bump or rattle the table. So far, the talk wasn't anything much. Mrs. Gribbell and Miss Sternum talked about the lovely spring weather and the remaining snow on the top of Pikes Peak. Miss Sternum said something about the school hike up to the top of Mount Pisgah, which Ruby learned was the name of the cone-shaped mountain she'd seen on her way into town.

"I've been to the top of Mount Sniffles," Ruby said, deciding to join the conversation.

"Mount Sneffels?" Miss Sternum corrected. "Down in the San Juan Mountains near Ouray?"

"Sniffles, Sneffels," Ruby said. "I only know Pa and I got caught in a thunderstorm up there, and we were sniffling for weeks."

Mary and Eloise giggled, but stopped when Mrs. Gribbell leaned forward and spoke. "My dear, it's highly unlikely that you've been to the top of a 14,000-foot mountain."

"That's exactly what Pa said!" Ruby smiled at the memory. " 'It's unlikely we're going to make it up those steep rocks before those clouds move in.' But we did, and we barely got off the peak before the first rain fell."

Miss Sternum looked warily at Mrs. Gribbell. "Ruby's had," she paused, "an adventuresome life."

At that moment, Maude poked her head over the backyard fence. Eloise and Mary leapt from their seats and ran to her.

"Young ladies!" Mrs. Gribbell frowned and called after them. "That animal needs to stay…"

Mary had already opened the gate, and Maude trotted over to the table and nosed into Ruby's plate.

"Shooo!" Mrs. Gribbell stood so suddenly she

tilted the table. Teacups, saucers, plates, and cookies slid onto the ground. Maude bucked and kicked, catching a front hoof in the bottom rungs of Mary's empty chair. Maude reared to shake off the chair and bumped the table on the underside. More plates jumped, and everyone scrambled to save what they could.

Ruby grabbed Maude's halter rope just as Maude rocked back with the chair still on her hoof. It caught Ruby in the knee, and she dropped the lead, doubling over, hopping and yelping in pain. Maude swung the chair up a second time, catching Ruby under her left eye. With one last effort, Maude shook the chair free. Ruby lunged and grabbed the end of the rope as Maude started off at a fast trot toward the gate.

The rope jerked Ruby off her feet and onto her face. She held on, bouncing and skidding and hollering for Maude to stop. The girls screamed and ran after Ruby—until Maude, safely away from the chair attack, slowed to a halt in the front yard of the house.

"Oh my goodness." Miss Sternum joined the girls, with Mrs. Gribbell following at her heels.

Ruby stood slowly, brushing the dirt from her yellow dress. She checked to make sure Maude was all right and assessed the damage to her knee. Blood streamed down the front of her shin and dripped red polka dots onto her new white shoes.

"Oh my!" Mrs. Gribbell clapped a hand over her mouth. Her eyes widened, and her face turned pale.

"Girls," Miss Sternum directed, "bring some soap and water and a bandage."

A few minutes later, Miss Sternum had Ruby's knee cleaned and wrapped. Ruby stood and hobbled a little. She felt her left eye swelling and pressed a hand to her upper cheek.

Miss Sternum brushed her hands together. "I imagine that finishes the afternoon."

Still a little shaken, Mrs. Gribbell nodded. "I certainly hadn't imagined an ending like this!"

Ruby felt genuinely bad about ruining Mrs. Gribbell's party. She still wanted to try the sugar cookies, and she'd only had one bite of her jam tart. Besides, Maude hadn't gotten to try any of the sweets. She wished she'd been able to put a cookie in her pocket. "I hope you'll invite us back," she said.

Seven

Ruby stitched the yellow dress and took it to the creek to wash. She dried it on a wire line behind the wood stove. Practically as good as new, Ruby thought. Her knee, however, needed a little explaining. And the eye. Ruby studied her swollen eye in the mirror. Her right eye still showed a bluish color around the rim, and the left eye was trying to catch up.

Pa sighed when he saw her. "It doesn't look like you made much headway on becoming a lady."

Ruby launched into a tale about the afternoon and how the chair had spooked Maude and the table tipped and ...

Pa scratched his whiskers thoughtfully. "Miss Sternum could be right. You need more than a little socialization."

"So-shu-li-zay-shun!" Ruby repeated the word back slowly. "What does that mean?"

"Taming," Pa said.

Ruby folded her arms across her chest. "Miss Sternum thinks I'm a wild animal?"

Pa laughed. "You're worse than a wild grizzly in a leg trap." He ruffled Ruby's hair.

A moment later he became serious, examining his hands in a way that Ruby knew meant he was thinking hard on something. "I just want to make sure I'm doing right by you. You might not always be happy roaming around the hills with your old Pa."

Ruby started to interrupt, but he waved her to silence. "I promised your mama I'd bring you up right, and you know how I feel about breaking promises."

Ruby knew. One time she'd promised to write a letter to Granny Oliver while Pa went into town for supplies. She'd chased butterflies instead. Pa's words still burned into her memory. "A promise is like a thread of trust between two humans. When a promise gets broken, that thread gets frayed. If you break too many promises, the strand separates, and there's no fixing it again."

Ruby's throat felt tight. She didn't see anything wrong with her upbringing. Besides she didn't know any other way to be. Pa had never been troubled about her upbringing before. Something had gotten into him since they'd come to Cripple Creek—since that Hawker man stole their things. Ruby decided she was going to be on her best behavior for a little while, so Pa wouldn't have to worry about her. She especially didn't want him to go too far down that "bringing her up right" line of thinking. That trail was one rocky path she did not want to follow.

* * *

On Monday, Ruby decided to wear her yellow dress to school. It would please Miss Sternum, and perhaps Miss Sternum would write Pa a good letter about it. She hoped the other girls would notice she was trying, too. She really hadn't meant to ruin the party. However, it did seem like a lot of trouble for Agnes's mother to set up a big table with all of those fancy cups and saucers and dishes just to eat a few sweets. Tin plates would have worked fine.

Ruby's thoughts were interrupted by a familiar voice. "You got a new dress," Josef said, as he and Franz caught up.

Franz jabbed Josef with his elbow and said, "She looks like one of our chickens."

"Our chickens don't wear boots."

Ruby walked faster, trying to leave the two pests behind, but they trotted along beside her. "I've got something for Maude," Josef said, pulling a carrot from his lunch pail.

"Where'd you get that?" Franz asked.

"From Old Man Johnson's root cellar."

Seeing the carrot, Maude pulled back on the lead and refused to move. Ruby waited impatiently while Maude chewed. Not to be outdone, Franz dug into his lunch and tore off a piece of pancake. Maude lipped it off his fingers and waited for more.

"It's time to go." Ruby pulled on Maude's rope and turned, nearly bumping into a short wiry man with black stringy hair and a jagged scar down one cheek.

"That's a fine critter you have there," the man said. "How much you want for her?"

Ruby glared at him. "What makes you think she's for sale?"

The man shrugged. "Seen her wandering around the school like she didn't have a home."

"She belongs to me and my Pa," Ruby said. *The nerve of this man wanting to buy Maude!*

"The mines is payin' plenty for good, stout stock."

Stout stock! What did he think Maude was? She would never sell Maude. And neither would Pa. "My donkey's not for sale."

The man snorted. "Darn shame. A donkey like that needs to be put to work."

The school bell rang. "Come on, Maude." She glanced back once and saw the awful man staring after her.

All morning Ruby worried about Maude, using any excuse she could think of to peek out the window and make sure Maude was all right. The rest of the time Ruby wiggled and squirmed in her desk. No matter which way she sat, the bones in her corset bodice poked, jabbed, and stabbed. It reminded her of the time she and Pa had helped a man with a broken leg. They'd taken branches and twine to fix the leg in place. Ruby didn't see the point in splinting up her ribs. They weren't injured.

"Miss Oliver," Miss Logan said. "Your mind does not appear to be on your lessons."

Ruby straightened in her seat to see if that would keep the corset stays from digging in. It worked for a few minutes, but then she started sagging and aching again. By lunch Ruby had a plan. She waited until most of the class had gone out. Then she tiptoed down the hall to the small room where she'd seen Miss Logan get a broom and dustpan. With a quick look around to make sure no one was watching, Ruby turned the knob and slipped into the janitor's closet. It only took her a few minutes to shimmy out of her dress, remove the corset, and shimmy back in. She stashed the corset behind a broom, grabbed her lunch, and walked back into the hall.

"What were you doing in there?" Roy O'Rourke leaned against the wall near the closet door.

Ruby didn't figure Roy really wanted to know. She ignored him and hurried down the hall and out the door. As she hopped down the steps, she felt as free as an air-borne eagle.

Ruby first thought she'd find Agnes and her friends and get to know them a little better, but when they saw her coming, they drew into a tight ring that looked to Ruby like wagons circling before an attack. Ruby decided her donkey would be much better company. She skipped past them to where Maude stood with a group of admirers—mostly younger students—who petted her and fed her nibbles from their lunches. Josef stood at the center, making sure everyone knew that he and Maude were already the best of friends.

Ruby patted Maude and sat down nearby. She opened her lunch and pulled out some bacon and a biscuit left over from breakfast. She was saving the nut butter for last. Pa didn't buy that very often.

A few feet away, Ruby noticed a girl sitting alone. She looked about the same age as Josef, with sandy-colored hair that was chopped off just below her ears. She was as bony as one of Maude's legs and wore a dress that made Ruby's old one look brand-new. Ruby wondered if she had anything in her lunch bucket and was about to find out when a shout erupted from the other side of the schoolyard.

Next, as if a pen full of piglets had been all squeezed at once, a loud squeal rose from where Agnes and her friends huddled. The girls pointed, and Agnes clapped a hand over her mouth. Ruby followed the pointing fingers—up, up, up. At the top of the flagpole, where the American flag usually hung, Ruby's corset flopped in the breeze like a dead snowshoe hare.

"What's that thing?" Josef turned his attention from Maude and joined the excitement. One by one, children stopped playing and looked up. Some of the older boys grouped together and started whispering. As Ruby crossed the schoolyard to get a better look, she heard Lester Ward say, "It looks just like my ma's, only she hangs it on a clothesline line, not on a flagpole."

Roy O'Rourke leaned against the side of the building with a wide grin on his face. Ruby spotted him and froze. She could walk over and wallop him, but then everyone would know the corset belonged to her. She'd have to explain to Miss Sternum what she was doing in the janitor's closet, and...

Lester made a beeline to Roy. He seemed to holler, "Do you know where *that* came from?"

Roy lifted his eyebrows and nodded his head in Ruby's direction. He didn't have to say a word. Lester's head swiveled, and the eyes of everyone on the playground pivoted to Ruby.

That does it! Ruby stomped over to where Roy stood, doubling her fists. She'd promised Pa she wouldn't fight, but that didn't mean she couldn't give Roy a good talking to. Jabbing her hands into her hips, she leaned forward, her nose almost touching his. "You've no right to hang my under-things up on that pole. They're private, private, private!"

Roy didn't say anything. He whistled through his teeth with a gleam of mischief dancing in his eyes. Ruby was about to break her promise to Pa and give him the poke in the mouth he deserved when an enormous dark shadow made a silhouette on the building in front of her. "What on earth is going on?"

Roy rolled his eyes upward and lifted his chin toward the top of the pole. Miss Sternum caught her breath. Ruby followed Miss Sternum's gaze, up, up, up. Miss Sternum seemed not to believe her eyes. Was that a corset where the flag should have been?

"It's Ruby's," Lester volunteered.

"Miss Oliver," she said sternly without taking her eyes off the top of the flagpole.

Ruby didn't have to be told she was in trouble. She headed for Miss Sternum's jail without so much as a "but."

Eight

Ruby sat at the bottom of the school steps fingering the new letter Miss Sternum had written. Maude stood nearby, ears tipped toward Ruby and eyes round with sympathy. "I sure hope Pa doesn't want to buy me any more new clothes. I've had enough trouble on account of the ones he just bought me."

Maude wuffled, a sound donkeys make to comfort their young.

"Maybe you and I should go traveling—just the two of us," Ruby continued. She turned the letter over and over, wondering how she was going to explain this one to Pa.

A small voice interrupted her thoughts. "Do you think Maude likes pickles?"

Ruby looked up and into the eyes of the girl she'd seen sitting by herself at lunchtime. A sprinkling of freckles dotted the girl's cheeks, and two front teeth were missing. "Who are you?" Ruby asked.

The girl answered with a rush of words. "Elizabeth Alexandria McAvery the third, but my Pa calls me Lizzybetty on account of my ma's name is Elizabeth and my grandma's, too, and she lives with us, and when someone says Elizabeth, everyone jumps, and so he decided I would be Lizzybetty, which makes my name too hard to say, so most people call me Lizzy."

Worn out from Lizzy explaining her name, Ruby considered whether or not Maude liked pickles. As far as she knew, Maude had never had one, but she supposed Maude would give it a try. In the last week, Ruby had seen Maude eat everything from sweet potatoes to onions.

Lizzy started talking again. "I hope Maude likes pickles because my Ma makes the best pickles in Cripple Creek, and she told me if I was real good, she'd pack me one in my lunch tomorrow, and I want Maude to have a bite, but she can't have the whole thing because Ma wouldn't like it, and neither would I because I love pickles and don't get them very often. Ma's trying to make them last until she can make some more, but first we have to wait until summer so we can get some cucumbers from down valley, and then we'll have to save some money for vinegar."

Lizzy took a deep breath. "Our credit's no good at the store no more, but I still want Maude to have a bite of my pickle because she's the only friend I got." Lizzy's lip quivered, and her eyes filled with tears. "And if Maude won't be my friend, I won't have nobody else." She sniffled and wiped her eyes with the back of her hand.

"Maude will be your friend," Ruby said. "I will, too."

The girl smiled, showing the gap between her teeth. "You will?"

Ruby nodded. "And you don't have to bring Maude food. She likes to be scratched almost as much as she likes eating. I'll show you her tickle spot."

Ruby rubbed Maude's belly near her front withers, and then she let Lizzy have a try. Maude responded with a low, throaty sound that caused Lizzy to giggle. "Does anyone else know about Maude's tickle spot?"

"No, it's a secret, just between you and me."

Lizzy stopped scratching and stepped away from Maude, giving her one last pat on the side of the neck. "I'd better get going."

Ruby waited for Lizzy to leave, but she stood staring at the ground, as if her feet were glued down.

"Is your house near here?" Ruby asked.

"Down yonder." Lizzy pointed south toward the area of town where Ruby and Pa lived.

"How come you're still here at school? Shouldn't you be at home?"

She shrugged, and Ruby hoped she wouldn't cry again. "Not supposed to talk about it."

"You can tell Maude anything," Ruby said, "and she won't tell a soul."

Lizzy glanced at Maude's probing eyes, trying to decide if she could be trusted. "Are you sure?"

"I'm sure." Ruby thought about all the times she had told Maude her deepest secrets and how much better she felt afterward.

Lizzy sidled up next to Maude and stood on tiptoes so she could whisper into her ear. "Pa's drunk again. Ma threw the skillet at him. He has a bump on his head bigger than an acorn squash."

Ruby pretended she hadn't heard as Lizzy lowered back down onto her heels and asked, "What does *decent* mean?"

Ruby had to think how to explain it. "It means honest and upright." She paused and added, "Respectable."

Lizzy stretched up to Maude's ear again. "Ma says if he doesn't get decent work pretty soon, she's going to pack up the family and move to Illinois where Grandma Alice and Grandpa Charlie live. And she's going to leave him here to drink himself to death."

Ruby thought Lizzy was finished, but in a final burst, she cried, "And that's why no one at school likes me. Pa spends all his time down at Johnny Nolan's Saloon, and what's worse, everybody in town knows it." Lizzy sniffled. "I don't want him to drink himself to death. He's the only Pa I've got."

Maude nosed Lizzy as if waiting for more, but that was all. Lizzy lowered herself back down on her heels and heaved a sigh as if a heavy burden had been lifted.

"I bet your Pa could get a job up in one of the mines," Ruby said. "They pay $3.00 a day."

Lizzy shook her head. "He's a prospertector and works for himself." She mispronounced *prospector*. "He wants to strike it rich on his own like Mr. Stratton."

Ruby knew about prospectors. She and Pa had sold candleholders to plenty of them. A miner worked for a big company, like the ones up Poverty Gulch, but prospectors did their own digging. They roamed the hills looking for places to stake a claim. Some walked around with crooked sticks they called divining rods and wherever those rods pointed, that's where they'd dig. Others just kept an eye out for anything that sparkled and tried to find its source. Mr. Stratton found his mine that way, and everybody knew that he struck it rich.

"Elizabeth Alexandria McAvery! You get yourself home, right now! Ma's worried sick." An older boy with freckles and sandy hair the color of Lizzy's walked toward them. "And Pa said I could whup you if you didn't listen."

Lizzy's eyes grew wide. "It's my brother, Franky." She scampered off, putting a safe distance between her and the older boy. Maude began to bray after her. Just before Lizzy disappeared, she turned and gave Ruby and Maude a quick wave.

Ruby watched her go. Then she thought about her own troubles. She'd never had a whuppin' and didn't plan to start now. She decided the best thing to do with Miss Sternum's letter was to go straight to the livery and give it to Pa face to face. That way he'd have plenty of time to think the situation over before he got home. And he'd go easy on her because she'd been honest. She'd remind him of that if she had to.

With Maude at her side, Ruby walked down First Street and left on Bennett to the El Paso Livery. Pa was in one of the stalls, currying a large ginger-colored horse with a golden mane. "Have you ever seen a prettier horse?" he asked Ruby as she squeezed in next to him. "This is Goldie," Pa continued. "She's our new boarder. Over here's her partner." Pa walked around to the next stall. "His name's Lightning."

Ruby saw immediately how he got his name. Lightning was black with a silvery mane. His tail hung almost to the ground, and he had a lively spark in his eyes. Pa showed her a few other horses, then asked, "What brings you here this time of day?"

Ruby fidgeted, then handed Pa the letter. He recognized the handwriting. "Don't suppose this is good news?"

"S'pose not." Ruby captured one of her "escaped" hairs and smoothed it behind one ear.

Pa tucked the letter into his back pocket. "I'll be home around supper, and we can talk about it then. Think you can stay out of trouble that long?"

Ruby nodded, feeling a little relieved Pa hadn't read the letter right then and there. She left the livery and wandered down Bennett with Maude, not really in a hurry to get home. As the Palace Drug came into view, Maude picked up her pace.

"There's no money for ice cream today," Ruby said firmly. She resigned herself to a contest of "tug and pull" to get Maude past the window.

Instead, Maude stopped, curled her upper lip and stretched out her neck. She yanked the lead rope free and trotted over to a gray-bearded man sitting on a bench near the drugstore entrance.

"Whoa, whoa!" The man dropped his pocketknife and the piece of wood he'd been carving and held up one arm protectively as Maude sniffed at his upper body and face. "Whoa," the man said again. He began to laugh, reaching out to Maude, rubbing her ears and scratching under her chin. Maude returned his affection with little nibbles and nuzzles.

Ruby stared. At first she thought the man might need some help fending off Maude. Now he seemed just fine. In fact, they both seemed just fine. Ruby felt a twinge of jealousy. She'd never seen Maude take to anyone so quickly.

Maude looked over at Ruby and blinked her round eyes as if wondering why Ruby wasn't as enthusiastic about meeting a new friend. When Ruby didn't respond, Maude trotted over and nudged her toward the bench.

"That was quite a howdy," the man said. "My name's Amos—Amos McGee."

"You've already met Maude," Ruby said, still feeling a little bristly. "I'm Ruby."

Amos reached down and picked up his pocketknife and the piece of notched pine. As he did, Ruby noticed Amos's wooden leg. It was fitted just below his right knee and tapered to a stump about the size of a table leg.

"I'm guessing the two of you are pretty tight," Amos continued as he tugged on his long, scraggly beard. "Can't say as I blame you."

"Tight as bark on a tree."

"Reminds me of Sylvia." A sad look passed over the old man's face. "The only girl I ever loved."

Ruby's curiosity got the best of her, and she moved closer. She felt a little more friendly. "Was

Sylvia your wife?"

Amos shook his head and set down his whittling. He hobbled off the bench to stroke Maude's ears again.

"Your mother?" Ruby continued.

"My heavens no," Amos laughed. "I loved Sylvia McGee twice as much as my mother. Nothing wrong with my ma, mind you, but Sylvia was nicer to be around."

Maude nosed Amos. "Just like my Sylvia." Amos chuckled again.

"Where is Sylvia now?" Ruby asked.

"She's a 'was,'" Amos said. "She *was* the best burro that ever lived. Strong as an ox and friendly as a kitten." He dug into his pocket for some change. "I have a hankerin' for some ice cream. How about you?"

Ruby hesitated. "Could I buy one for Maude, too?"

Amos pressed a few coins into Ruby's hand. "There's enough to buy three."

Ruby hurried inside and returned with three penny licks, one for each of them. Ruby handed Amos an ice cream and sat beside him on the bench, holding one ice cream out for Maude. Maude swept her tongue around the inside of the shallow dish and nosed Amos for more.

Amos took a small taste, then tipped the rest of

his penny lick toward Maude as he continued his story. "When Sylvia started to stumble, I should have known what was comin'. We was workin' down under at the Molly Kathleen. First she wandered off the tracks, then started bumping the walls of the tunnel. I helped her the best I could 'til the boss found out. 'Got no use for a blind burro,' he told me."

Amos was quiet for a moment, and his eyes brimmed with tears. "What happened?" Ruby felt a little snuffly, too.

"Oh, I pleaded with the boss man to let Sylvia live, and he let me take her home. I watched her careful and made sure she was fed, but one day she disappeared. Just like that. Gone. Probably stumbled into an abandoned mine shaft or wandered into the hills and got ate up by mountain lions."

Ruby shuddered at the thought. "Didn't her eyes get better?"

Amos shook his head. "She'd been down in the mines too long. That's what happens to mine burros. After years without any light, they go blind. There's no help for it."

Ruby pulled Maude to her and patted her neck. She couldn't imagine Maude going blind. And she couldn't imagine her living underground without the fresh smells of pine and sagebrush and the colors of the wildflowers speckling the hills in the springtime.

Ruby wondered about Amos. Did he lose his leg in the mines? How did he make a living when he couldn't mine anymore? She'd only known him for an hour, but already he felt like an old friend.

As if he had read Ruby's mind, Amos said. "All in all, I can't complain. After the dynamite explosion that took my leg, I got a letter from back East. My old uncle died and left me enough to keep me going." He winked at Ruby. "And buy ice cream for my new girlfriends, too."

Ruby smiled and took the empty penny licks back into the drugstore and placed them on the soda fountain bar. A man wearing an apron stood behind it, pulling a shiny lever to add carbonated water to some cherry syrup to make a soda. Her mouth watered as she read the other flavors: strawberry, lemon, sarsaparilla.

"Would you like one?" the man asked, reaching for a glass.

Ruby shook her head. Out of the corner of her eye, she saw Amos stand and stretch. He scratched Maude's ears again and started to hobble west on Bennett. Ruby hurried from the drugstore to say good-bye. "Will you be here again?"

"Only if my two new girlfriends come by to see me."

Ruby watched Amos hobble away using one

crutch to help him balance on his bad leg. While she'd been talking to him, she'd forgotten all about the latest letter from Miss Sternum. Now that Amos was gone, a slow dread crept in. What would Pa say about the second letter? Worse, what had Miss Sternum written?

Nine

Pa didn't seem perturbed at all when he got home from the livery. He hugged Ruby the same as always and handed her the folded paper. "You make sure Miss Sternum gets this tomorrow." He whistled as he removed his boots and set about frying up a piece of ham he'd come home with.

Pa's cheerfulness made Ruby nervous. Either Miss Sternum's letter wasn't as bad as she thought, or Pa had decided to go right along with whatever Miss Sternum had suggested. Ruby was pretty sure it wasn't the first thing. Her fingers itched to see what Pa had written, but she decided it would be better to wait.

On the way to school the next morning, when Ruby was sure no one was around to see, Ruby read

Pa's reply. "I will consider your suggestions and discuss it with Ruby."

That didn't sound so bad. Whatever it was, Pa would talk it over with her first. Ruby walked a few more steps. She almost folded the letter up, but then she stopped. *What suggestions?* She had to know. Ruby turned the letter over, sure that if she put her mind to it, she could make sense of the handwriting.

Slowly, she figured out the code. It was like Pa's writing only loop-de-looped together. She read, "School of Dramatic Art, music, oil painting, decorative needlework, el-o-cu-tion." *Elocution.* Ruby paused and practiced pronouncing the word. Miss Sternum's letter ended with, "Perhaps one of these would interest Ruby?"

Ruby folded the letter and started walking again. She knew for sure that decorative needlework wasn't going to interest her. She already knew how to mend and patch. As for music, she and Pa knew lots of trail songs, and some of them they could sing in two parts.

Elocution. Ruby rolled the word on her tongue. *Elocution.* The word worried her all day. After school, Ruby headed straight to the Masonic Temple where she'd seen the sign School of Dramatic Art. Ruby skimmed down the sign and came to the words, "Elocution—the latest system of instruction." This was the place.

Ruby tied Maude to a streetlamp and opened the door. The entryway was large and empty. Ruby wanted to holler and test for an echo, but decided she'd better not. She heard faint voices and tiptoed across the polished hardwood floor to a room with a heavy door that was slightly ajar. Ruby leaned forward to listen.

"Lovely, lovely." A melodious voice called out, followed by brisk hand clapping. "Now this time, you must round your *o*'s and close up your *t*'s." The speaker demonstrated with a "t-t-t" sound that reminded Ruby of a woodpecker tapping a tree. The students began again, reciting a poem by Emily Dickinson that Ruby knew by heart. It was from a book her mama had given Pa.

Ruby concentrated, remembering the last time Pa had read it to her.

Have you got a brook in your little heart;
Where bashful flowers blow;
And blushing birds go down to drink;
And shadows tremble so?

Ruby melted into the door, daydreaming of little brooks and running barefoot in the grass. Her weight slowly shifted, the hinges creaked, and the door swung inward. Ruby lost her balance and stumbled into the room. Five young girls stood in a line in front of a row of straight-backed chairs and stared at her.

A very tall woman wearing a yellow tea gown adorned with white lace greeted Ruby. "Good afternoon. I'm Madame Fleur. May I help you?" The woman spoke with a French accent, each word round and flowing.

Ruby curtsied, hoping it was the right thing to do. "I was listening to the poem," she said. "It made me homesick."

Madame Fleur nodded for the students to sit. The girls, slightly older than Ruby, obeyed, arranging their dresses neatly. "Are you interested in elocution?" the instructor asked.

"I don't reckon I am," Ruby said, "since I don't know what it is."

The girls shifted in their chairs and tittered behind their gloved hands.

Madame Fleur smiled patiently and said in the same melodious voice. "You've just heard an excellent example." With a swoop of her hand, she motioned toward the class. "Elocution, my dear, is the management of voice and gesture." When Ruby wrinkled her brow in confusion, she continued. "The art," which she pronounced *aught*, "of speaking—and pronouncing—every—single— word—clearly."

"It's learning how to talk?" Ruby breathed a sigh

of relief. "I guess I won't be needing that. I can talk just fine." She glanced over at the girls, wondering why they were giggling.

"Young ladies." Madame Fleur turned to the girls with a look of reprimand. "All of art," she paused, "is nature in its more refined form."

Ruby liked this. Nature was something she understood. "I don't think you can improve on nature," she said. "Everything under God's blue sky is perfect already." That's the way Pa had told it, anyway.

"Quite so," Madame Fleur said. "But we are in agreement, are we not, that sometimes it is humans who need a little, mmm, polish?"

Ruby looked down at the white shoes she'd been wearing to please her pa. They were scuffed and dirty, and the bows were sagging. "I guess so, but I don't see much point in buffing up something that hurts your feet."

The girls burst out laughing.

Ruby frowned. She was starting to get put out with their bad manners.

"Young ladies," Madame Fleur scolded them again. "When you laugh, it must not sound like donkeys hee-hawing."

As if on cue, Maude began to bray loudly. The sound carried from the street and in through an open window in the elocution room. The girls slapped their knees and began to imitate Maude. One of them laughed so hard, she had to grab on to the girl next to her to keep from falling out of her chair.

In the midst of this, Madame Fleur began to bray like a donkey as well, but her hee-haw sounded like a bird, running up and down a musical scale in song. Swinging her arms gracefully, Madame Fleur moved around the room. Every few steps, she kicked up her legs in a donkey-like fashion and stopped. She hee-hawed and started prancing again, the skirt of her frilly dress swinging.

The other girls joined in. They formed a line and followed Madame Fleur, weaving and curving around the room in rhythm. They hee-hawed and giggled every few steps.

Ruby decided it was time to leave. She hurried out to the street and untied Maude. "I learned all about elocution," she said, "and if Pa decides to send me here for more learning, he's going to have to start feeding me hay."

Maude replied, but instead of a loud and impatient bray, this one sounded nice, like a melody. Ruby wondered if Maude had been eavesdropping.

Ten

The next morning, as they neared school, Maude shot ahead toward a small group of children gathered by the schoolyard fence. Lizzy McAvery pushed to the front of the group. "I'm going to feed her first." She held half a pickle on her open palm. Maude lipped it and chewed, nuzzling her for more. A wide grin spread across Lizzy's face.

"It's my turn," Josef said, elbowing forward. Several other children had treats ready to feed Maude, and they crowded around wanting to be next.

Lizzy ran to catch up with Ruby. "Maude liked the pickle!" she said. They climbed the front steps of the school together.

At the top, Ruby stopped to look back down Warren Avenue. About half a block away, leaning against the sideboards of a wagon, was the same stringy-haired man she'd seen a few days earlier. He was talking to a large man with his back turned to her. Something about the man looked familiar.

"You look like you seen a Tommyknocker," Lizzy said.

Ruby knew about Tommyknockers. They were little ghosts who caused mischief for the miners by moving tools and blowing out candle flames. "It could be a Tommyknocker, or something worse," she said, trying to figure out where she'd seen the other man. If only he'd turn around.

Ruby shook off her worries. It was probably her imagination, but before she entered the school, she checked to see where Maude was.

When Ruby sat down at her desk, she was surprised to see Miss Sternum at the front of the room next to Miss Logan. "Class," Miss Sternum began, "I've come to tell you about the spring hike up Mount Pisgah."

Excitement tingled through the class.

"As long as the weather holds, it will be on Saturday, April 25."

Ruby brightened. Any hike pleased her. And it would please Maude too. In fact, now that she wasn't walking miles on the trails but was getting lots of treats, Maude was getting plump. A hike would do her good. Ruby waved her hand in the air. "Is it all right if Maude comes with us?"

Miss Sternum frowned and glanced out the window.

"She won't do no harm," Roy O'Rourke said.

Ruby glared at Roy. She didn't know if she wanted him coming to Maude's defense. And she didn't like the way he'd been bringing treats to Maude like the other children. Maybe Maude had forgiven Roy, but Ruby was taking her time.

Miss Sternum heaved a sigh. "I shall consider it. In the meantime, please tell your families about the upcoming date. I will provide more information as the day nears."

Ruby forgot about her problems with Miss Sternum and counted days until the hike. April 25 was only two Saturdays away. She couldn't wait to tell Pa, and if she talked it up real good, it might give him the itch to go traveling again.

After school, Ruby walked to the livery to tell him about the hike, but he was delivering a load of feed up Poverty Gulch. She thought about waiting but decided to walk down Bennett to look for Amos. The bench outside the drugstore was empty, so Ruby continued down the street, content to tell Maude about the hike. "You're going to love it," Ruby said. "That's if Miss Sternum lets you go."

Maude seemed to like the idea and trotted ahead. At the next corner, she halted. Her ears straightened, and she swiveled them left and right. Ruby caught up and paused next to Maude, listening. Faintly muffled sobs came from somewhere nearby. Ruby encouraged Maude forward. At their feet, two arms and a head poked out of a dress that had been pulled down over two knobby knees and tucked under like a tent with hair. Nothing else showed.

Maude sniffed and nudged the cloth lump until a tear-streaked face appeared. Ruby gasped, "Lizzy! What's wrong?"

Lizzy stood shakily and wrapped her arms around Maude's neck. She wiped her eyes and stuttered, "It's m-my pa again. He's over at the bar, and I got to go get him and bring him home before Ma f-finds out."

Ruby looked kitty-corner across the street at Johnny Nolan's Saloon and patted Lizzy's shoulder.

"If he comes home l-lickered up, I don't know what my m-ma will do," Lizzy sniffled. "He'll listen to me. I know he will," She wiped her eyes with her sleeve. "But ..."

Ruby waited.

"I'm too sc-scared to go in there." She burst into tears again, burying her face in her hands.

Maude bumped Ruby as if to ask her to do something. Ruby glanced across the street again. She didn't think she should go into a saloon. Pa always stayed away from them and warned Ruby to stay away, too.

Lizzy gulped air. "I'll j-just have to go h-home without him."

Ruby pondered. What could be so hard about going into Johnny Nolan's, finding Lizzy's pa, and coming back out again? "I'll go get him for you," she said. "I'll have him out of there in no time."

"You will?" Lizzy's face brightened.

"I will." Ruby started across Bennett with Maude clopping along behind. She glanced over her shoulder at Lizzy. "I'll be right back."

"Wait!" Lizzy ran to catch up.

Outside the bar door, Ruby could hear laughter, bottles clanking, and loud talk. Ruby took a deep breath. "Does your pa have a name?"

"Joe," Lizzy said. "Joe McAvery."

"You wait here," Ruby said. "I'll go in and ask for him. It won't take long."

Lizzy shook her head. "I'm going in with you." She puffed herself up bravely. "I'm not scared anymore."

Ruby decided that it might be helpful to have Lizzy with her, in case Joe McAvery didn't want to leave. She grabbed Lizzy's hand and stepped in, pausing for a moment to let her eyes adjust to the dim light. The noise of the drinkers swelled around her, and the room smelled like sweat, alcohol, and cigar smoke.

Lizzy stood on tiptoes and whispered into Ruby's

ear. "There he is." She squeezed Ruby's hand. As if that were a signal, the customers, gripping thimble-shaped glasses and mugs of ale, stopped drinking, and the bartender quit pouring. Everyone stared.

Ruby cleared her throat. "We've come for Lizzy's pa." It sounded more like a frog croaking than words. She wondered if anyone had understood.

The bartender set down his bottle. A bar stool creaked. Ruby rolled her eyes in the direction that Lizzy had pointed. A man wearing a dirty denim jacket lay slumped over a small round table at the side of the room. One hand was curled around an empty glass.

"Lizzy's pa? Who might that be?" the bartender asked.

"He's over there, sir," Lizzy peeped. "Joe McAvery."

A few men grumbled. A tall man, sitting at the bar said, "You girls don't belong here. Go on home."

Ruby bristled. "Let's get your pa." Still gripping Lizzy, she started for the table where Mr. McAvery was slumped.

"I've never seen him like this before," Lizzy whispered. "Is he all right?"

Ruby didn't have any idea. She'd never been in a bar before or seen anyone drunk. Now she knew why Pa had steered away from saloons. Some of the men looked shifty, and all of them looked unwashed. A spittoon sat at the end of the bar.

"Pa?" Lizzy dropped Ruby's hand and gently shook his shoulder.

The hunched-over man exploded, sitting up abruptly and lashing out with his left arm, swinging at anything in his path. Ruby grabbed Lizzy and stumbled backward. She bumped a table, tipping over a tall, narrow bottle. It rolled to the edge, teetered, and fell.

The room erupted in a loud argument. "You girls get on out! Leave the man alone!" a man hollered.

"Let them take Joe home," a sympathetic voice shouted.

"McAvery can make up his own mind," someone else said.

"Don't look to me like he's too clear-headed right now." A round of raucous laughter ripped through the room.

"Maybe we should go," Ruby said to Lizzy. Joe McAvery had slumped back down on the table, moaning and resting his head in his arms.

Tears glistened in Lizzy's eyes. "I can't leave him here like this." She shook him again. "Pa, Pa, you have to come home."

While she was shaking him, the tall man from the bar left his stool and walked over. He lifted Lizzy by the back of her dress and dangled her above the rolling wine bottle. "Time to git."

"Leave her alone!" Angrily, Ruby kicked at the

back of the tall man's legs. His knees buckled, and he lurched forward, dropping Lizzy as he reached for balance.

As Lizzy scrambled up, a mustached man appeared and swung at the tall man. Ruby yanked Lizzy out of the way and ducked to miss the blow. They huddled against the wall as more men joined the fight, cursing loudly and swinging clenched fists. Like water bursting a dam, the entire room exploded into a full-blown brawl with everyone shoving, shouting, smacking, punching, and yelling.

Everyone except Joe McAvery. Ruby heard his raspy snores above the noisy fight. "Let's go," she said, tightening her grip on Lizzy's hand. "If Pa finds out that I've been in a saloon fight, he's going to use me for moosequatch bait!"

They inched their way along the wall toward the door. A man pivoted and punched another man holding a full whiskey bottle. The bottle flew out of his hand toward Ruby, drenching her dress and spilling liquor on her shoes as it hit the floor.

A loud braying came from the front door of the saloon, and Maude clomped in. Her complaining rose above the noise of the brawl as she reached the center of the room, nosing between the fighting men. Slowly, the scuffle ceased.

Ruby and Lizzy stepped around overturned tables and broken glass to get to Maude. Lizzy crooned, "It's all right, Maude. Nobody's fighting anymore." She clung to Maude like a leaf to a tree.

Ruby wasn't so sure that everything was all right. The saloon looked worse than their tent looked after a bear had ripped into it. And the customers looked as if they'd been mauled. All around the room, men dabbed at bloody lips and swollen cuts with neck scarves and handkerchiefs. Their clothes were torn and sopped with alcohol, and one of them had been knocked out cold.

The bartender's head poked up from behind the bar. He didn't seem at all surprised to see a full-grown donkey in the middle of the room. He came around and began righting the tables and chairs. "That's enough excitement for today," he said. "You boys help me load up this little girl's pa." He took off his derby and turned it upside down on one of the tables. "And you can put some cash in this here hat to pay for the damage."

Two men lifted Joe McAvery and hauled him over to the center of the room. They slung him over Maude's back as if he were a gunnysack of potatoes. "You girls think you can handle him from here?"

Ruby nodded and led Maude to the door. They wiggled through, with Lizzy tucking and folding her Pa's legs to make him fit. When they reached the street, Ruby drew in a long breath of fresh air. Nothing had ever smelled better.

"We got him! We got Pa." Lizzy grinned, showing the space between her front teeth. She pulled her pa's legs on one side of Maude, and then ran around to pull on his arms until he was perfectly balanced.

Ruby didn't recover as quickly. As she tugged on Maude's lead to get her going, something caught her eye. Down the street, outside the post office, a gray horse stood swishing its tail. There was something familiar about the horse, but at first she couldn't place it. Then it hit her. Jake Hawker's horse!

Ruby needed to find her pa. Pronto. If only Lizzy could wait a couple of minutes while she ran to the livery for help. She glanced at Mr. McAvery. It didn't look like he was going anywhere. "Lizzy…"

At that moment, Jake Hawker stepped out of the post office and squinted into the afternoon sun. He walked straight to his horse, climbed on, and rode east toward the Midland Terminal.

Ruby's mind raced. If she didn't do something fast, he'd be gone. As she watched the gray horse sway, she spotted Miss Sternum's bicycle, leaning near the door of Pearce Pharmacy. Ruby ran toward the conveyance, shouting over her shoulder to Lizzy. "Can you manage on your own for a few minutes?"

Lizzy nodded dumbly and took hold of Maude's rope. Ruby grabbed the bicycle, and without a hint about how to ride, she swung a leg over and perched on the seat. She pulled the skirt of her dress out of the way and tried to get her feet on the pedals. The bicycle wobbled and toppled. On the second try, Ruby managed to keep her balance and roll forward an inch or two. On the third try, the front wheel dipped down into a hole in the street. The bicycle lurched to a stop and Ruby flew off.

Miss Sternum came out of the store and shrieked. She marched over to where Ruby lay beside the fallen bicycle. "Whatever are you doing with my transport?" A frown pinched her face.

"I ... you see ... um ..." Ruby scrambled up. She was saved when Miss Sternum noticed Maude and Lizzy, standing a few feet away.

"What *are* you girls doing?" Miss Sternum's gaze passed from Ruby to Lizzy to Maude. Her nose wrinkled as the odor of Ruby's whiskey-soaked dress floated upward. Stiffly, she asked, "Have you girls been drinking?"

Out of the corner of her eye, Ruby tried to keep track of Hawker. She watched as his horse wove through the clump of people near the front of the train depot and disappeared up Fifth. She barely heard Miss Sternum say, "I think it's time I had a little chat with your fathers."

"My Pa's right here," Lizzy said. A long, loud groan came from the body draped over Maude's back as Joe McAvery tried to lift his head. After a feeble effort, he flopped down again, dangling like a worn-out rag doll.

Miss Sternum leaned forward, adjusted her glasses, and squinted at Mr. McAvery. For a long moment, she said nothing.

"And we're taking him home right now!" Ruby said quickly. She didn't wait for Miss Sternum to recover. She grabbed Maude's lead rope and started down Bennett, jogging a little faster than she should have with Mr. McAvery in tow.

"Slow down," Lizzy said. "You're going to lose my pa." She trotted alongside Maude, pulling at arms and legs to keep Joe McAvery from bouncing off.

Eleven

Ruby had never seen Pa this angry. Not even when she'd started the tent on fire. The bacon grease had spilled onto the lantern and then—poof! That pretty much described Pa right now. He was ready to explode. Word had spread down Bennett Avenue and jumped like a wild flame into the El Paso Livery. The brawl, the donkey, the girl who looked like Ruby. Pa had heard it all, and he'd come home right away to see if it was true.

The cabin was silent, except for the creaking of the floor as Pa paced back and forth in front of the cook stove. He turned at the cabin door and started back across, stopping briefly to lift the lid on the stew pot, stir, clap it back down, and start up again. "I should have listened to your Granny Oliver. She told me I needed a woman to help raise you." He spun again.

Ruby sat on a chair by the table, turning her head from one side to the other as Pa paced. She thought about the time they'd seen a caged raccoon. The coon had moved from one side to the other, back and forth, and never rested. Just like Pa now. Ruby steeled herself for a long evening.

"In a *saloon*!" Pa spat out the word like it was poison. "Mixing with all of those low-lifers and whiskey-drinking good-for-nothings."

"But Pa ..."

"There's no excuse for it. I've tried hard to raise you up right."

Ruby glanced out the west window at the disappearing sun.

"Worst of all," Pa continued. "I've failed your mother. If she had any idea you were spending your time in saloons ..." He stirred the stew again and slammed down the lid. "And I promised her I'd raise you up proper."

Ruby didn't see that she'd been spending much time in saloons. Pa made it sound like she stopped at Nolan's after school every day to guzzle one drink after another. She folded her arms across her chest. "You never cared about proper before." She jutted out her lower lip. "You used to like me just fine the way I am."

Pa kept pacing. "Smelling like whiskey and cigar

smoke? I should have settled you in school a long time ago! Should have done a lot of things a long time ago."

Feeling worse, Ruby pleaded. "Pa, you and me, we're partners. I don't need proper. I don't need school."

Pa lifted the stew pot lid and grabbed the spoon. He waved it, throwing bits of liquid into the air as he spoke. "You need school, and you need proper, and," he gave the spoon one last shake, "you need a mother."

Ruby inhaled quickly, catching a whiff of the alcohol on her clothes. "A mother!" If she'd been fragile, she would have fainted dead away. Instead, she readied herself for a good fight.

Pa stirred the stew and started pacing again, but this time a little more slowly. His shoulders relaxed, and he stroked his beard thoughtfully. It was as if he'd settled something that had been gnawing on him for a long time. "A mother," he repeated. "I don't care where she comes from or what she looks like as long as she knows proper. As long as she can give you the upbringing I promised your ma."

"Pa ..." All of Ruby's resolve to fight fizzled. "You've brought me up just fine."

He picked up his pacing speed again. "I will. That's exactly what I'll do. The next single woman I meet that knows proper is going to be your mother."

A dizzy feeling washed over Ruby. She grabbed a hold of the seat of her chair to keep from falling off. "Pa ..."

A rap on the door interrupted the conversation. Ruby sprang from her chair. *Don't let it be who I think it might be!* She leaned her back against the rough wood and spread her arms to block him from opening the door. "Pa, we don't need company. We haven't had supper yet."

Pa's frown moved Ruby aside, and he flung open the door. Ruby gulped, remembering Pa's words, "The next single woman I meet that knows proper is going to be your mother." Framed in the entrance, standing as stiff as a lamppost, stood Miss Sternum. Her lips made a thin, serious line across the lower part of her face.

"Come in," Pa said politely. He stepped out of the way so she could enter.

Miss Sternum took a tentative step into the cabin and glanced around the room. Ruby imagined every speck of unswept dust magnified to the size of Pikes Peak under her gaze. "Please sit down." Pa motioned to the chair where Ruby had been sitting.

"I won't be staying long." She sat and carefully folded her hands in her lap. Pa pulled up the chair opposite and leaned forward, arms crossed on the red-checked tablecloth. It looked as if he intended to concentrate fully on what Miss Sternum had to say.

Ruby plunked down on her cot. She desperately wanted to escape, but she was afraid Miss Sternum would turn the facts all topsy-turvy, and Ruby wanted to be here to set the record straight.

After a long, quiet moment of shifting uncomfortably in the straight-backed chair, Miss Sternum began. "I'm afraid I've come here to report some rather unladylike behavior on the part of your daughter." Miss Sternum said "unladylike" as if it were a handkerchief that needed to be laundered.

Pa glanced at the cot. "Ruby and I were just discussing this very thing."

"Well, then I do not need to elaborate on the facts."

Ruby scanned her vocabulary for the word *elaborate*. She guessed it meant to gush out all the details. It was probably a good thing Miss Sternum didn't plan to get wordy.

"However," Miss Sternum continued, "because of the seriousness of the situation, I thought it called for a visit in person." She paused. "This afternoon's events and other incidents, have led me to believe that Ruby is having a, mmm, difficult adjustment to a, mmm, more civilized life."

Civilized! Ruby wiggled, doubting very much that civilized was something she wanted to adjust to. She watched her Pa nod and smile. Then she started to worry. What if Pa did what he said he would do?

What if he decided to marry Miss Sternum!

Ruby studied the principal as if seeing her for the first time. Her high cheekbones were a bit sharp and angular, but the touch of red rouge softened them. Everything else, Ruby supposed, was as it should be: shiny black hair swept up, twisted, and pinned; spectacles in place; and not a thing untidy about her clothing. Miss Sternum looked very proper and almost attractive. Almost. Ruby shook the thought from her mind. *Pa wouldn't. Pa couldn't.*

When the talk ended, Pa said, "Allow me to escort you home, Miss Sternum. I believe it's getting dark."

Miss Sternum seemed a little flustered, the red of her cheeks spreading. "I have my conveyance."

"I'd feel much better if I knew you made it home safely."

Miss Sternum blushed again. "I thank you very much." She allowed Pa to follow her to the door. He opened it and, with a sweep of his hand, bowed and ushered her out. "The stew's hot," he said over his shoulder as he closed the door behind them.

Ruby stared at the doorknob. She waited for a minute, then tiptoed across the room and stepped out into the twilight. She could see the shapes of Pa and Miss Sternum. With the bicycle between them, they looked like a two-headed contraption fading away in the dusk.

Ruby heard a clop clop clop and looked over as Maude ambled toward the cabin. Ruby scratched Maude's ears and looked up into the steel gray sky. "We're in trouble, Maude," Ruby said. "We're in big, big trouble."

Twelve

Ruby didn't realize how huge the trouble was until the next morning. Pa stood at his shaving mirror and snipped at the corners of his mustache, whistling and humming softly. "What are you doing?" she asked.

"Thought I'd walk you to school this morning." Pa had on a clean shirt and had buffed his boots to a shine you could almost see your reflection in.

Pa whistled all the way to the school steps and lingered, looking around as if he'd lost something. Ruby couldn't figure out why, until she saw Miss Sternum peek from her office window. Pa tipped his hat and smiled at her. Miss Sternum gave a quick wave and disappeared.

The next day, the same thing happened, except this time Miss Sternum came outside and walked down the steps. Pa removed his hat. "Has my little girl been behaving?"

Little girl! Ruby felt as if someone had cut ten inches off her legs. Miss Sternum smiled at Ruby and then at her Pa. "I believe her behavior has improved greatly."

Ruby didn't see that she'd been behaving much differently. Although she *had* been staying out of saloons.

"There's a dance Friday night at the Klover Klub," Pa said. "It would be my pleasure to escort you there."

Miss Sternum nodded in a businesslike way. "I shall consider it."

Ruby figured that was Miss Sternum's way of saying yes. On Friday evening, she watched Pa shave and wash up. She wrinkled her nose. "What's that smell?"

A moment later, she recognized the bottle of toilet water Grandma Oliver had mailed him last Christmas. As far as Ruby knew, it had been stuffed at the bottom of their saddle packs. She hadn't known him to use it. Until now.

Pa turned to Ruby. "Do I look all right?"

Ruby thought maybe he needed a little dirt on his shirt or maybe a soot smudge on his face. That would be the Pa she was used to. "You look clean," she said.

Pa smiled. "If I'm not fancy enough, I'll have to make up for it with my charm."

"You've never worried about fancy before," Ruby said.

"You've got to look your best if you're trying to impress someone."

Pa was trying to impress Miss Sternum? Ruby couldn't believe her ears. He was taking this whole thing far too seriously. "Are you leaving me here all alone?" Ruby asked.

Pa tugged on her braid, then used the tip to tickle her neck. "You're the one that's been telling me you're grown up, and besides, Maude's right outside." He placed his hat on his head and left the cabin, humming.

Ruby followed him out the door. "He'll come to his senses soon," she told Maude. "One evening with Miss Sternum, and it will all be over."

The next night, Ruby wasn't so sure. After Pa left to escort Miss Sternum to the theater, she sat down on the front step and watched the moon come up. "We've got to figure out what to do before Pa does something he might regret." Maude perked her ears attentively and nosed Ruby.

"If Pa needs to find me a mother, he ought to be courting someone who likes to travel." She tried to imagine Miss Sternum riding her bicycle over La Veta Pass. "Or at least someone who likes camping."

For the first time in her life, Ruby didn't get any comfort from Maude. "I don't suppose Amos will be down at the drugstore this time of night." She thought hard about who she might be able to talk to. Then she remembered a sign on the side of Slusher's Grocery down on Bennett.

"Come on, Maude." Ruby started up the hill toward town.

Ruby had never been on Bennett Avenue after dark. During the day, it was filled with freight wagons and delivery carts, but at night, carriages pulled by prancing horses filled the street. On the boardwalk, ladies in fancy dresses and cloaks walked on the arms of men wearing top hats and tails. Small groups of people stood talking outside saloons and gambling halls.

Ruby stood at the corner of Fourth Street and Bennett, staring at the five stories of the partly built National Hotel. According to Amos, the hotel was going to have a barbershop with five chairs and a Turkish bath in the basement. When Ruby had asked about turkeys taking baths, Amos laughed and explained that it was a large room for steam baths and massages. Then he had added, "I suppose it's only for rich people like Myron Stratton, but just once, I'd like to try it."

Ruby thought a good hike and a dip in the creek would work just as well. She turned west on Bennett and detoured around the Butte Concert Hall. That's where Pa and Miss Sternum would be, and she didn't want to run into them. Ruby looked through windows and open doors where people laughed and gambled. The noises gurgled together, and soon she was daydreaming about mountain streams and wide-open spaces.

Before Ruby realized it, she'd reached the grocery. A light shone in one of the upstairs windows, and she heard footsteps coming down the steps toward her. With no time to move, a door flung open, and a woman wearing a sparkling evening dress stumbled into Maude.

"Gracious sakes, what kind of an animal is this?"

"I'm sorry ma'am," Ruby said. "It's my donkey, Maude."

The woman turned to her gentleman friend and began to laugh. "Do you think that's what Madam Estelle meant when she said we would make the acquaintance of someone new and unusual?"

The gentleman chuckled. He gripped the woman's arm and pulled her to him, staring down into her eyes. "Let's see if her readings on other things are true."

Ruby looked past the clutching couple to a sign. "Mme Estelle, Clairvoyant and Healer: Consultation, One Flight Up. "

"Excuse me," Ruby interrupted. "Is Madam

Estelle really a fortune-teller?"

Keeping her eyes locked on her gentleman friend, the woman said, "I certainly hope so." Still holding the woman tightly, the man spun her back onto his arm, and the two disappeared into the night.

Ruby reread the sign, taking a deep breath. "If there's something bad going to happen, it's better to know about it." Ruby tied Maude to a lamppost and climbed the narrow, dark stairs up to the second floor. At the landing, she knocked, and a low voice invited her to enter.

"Healing or seeing?" an older woman sitting behind a small table inquired.

"A little of both, I guess," Ruby said. She plunked into a chair opposite Madam Estelle. The seer's glittery gown sparkled in the lamplight, and a large shiny pendant hung from her neck.

"Is someone ill?" the madam asked.

Ruby considered this and nodded. "My pa," she said. "He's lovesick."

If Madam Estelle was amused, she didn't show it. "That," she said, "is a complicated thing to cure."

Ruby frowned. "I guess, then, I'd like to have some seeing."

Madam Estelle leaned forward. "First, do you have the money to pay?" Ruby shook her head. The fortune-teller looked her over for a moment. "Since you appear to be in great distress, I will do the reading for free."

Ruby exhaled in relief as Madam Estelle reached for her hand. She watched in fascination as the woman ran a long, painted fingernail over the lines and creases in her palm. "Hmmmm … Ahhhhhh …" The expression on the woman's face changed from a look of concentration to a deep frown of worry.

"Oh my." She lay Ruby's hand down on the table. "The lines are dark and threatening." Madam Estelle paused. "I see many things—flames, disaster, tragedy."

It was Ruby's turn to frown. "What kind of a disaster?"

Madam Estelle took Ruby's hand again and studied it. "The lines are too faint. The meaning is unclear."

Ruby leaned over and squinted at her palm, trying to make out what the seer was talking about. To her, the creases looked like trails and river forks.

There was a knock on the door. Madam Estelle dropped Ruby's hand and tapped the table with her long fingernails. "Your time is up."

"But …" Ruby's mind swam with questions.

The seer gave Ruby one last sympathetic look and urged her out. "I must attend to my paying customers."

Ruby rose and left the room, passing the next customer in the doorway. She clomped down the stairs. "Come on," she said to Maude when she reached the street. "We've got to figure out a way to put out the flames of love before there's a big disaster."

Thirteen

On Monday, Ruby was tired of all the attention Miss Sternum was getting from Pa. It was time to get a little for herself. She rubbed her cheeks until they turned red and clutched her stomach, moaning loudly. She wished there was some way to make her temperature go up, but since the weather had warmed, Pa hadn't been building a morning fire.

"I've never known you to be weedy," Pa responded. "Weedy" was what Pa called acting sick without a reason.

"I'm weedy now," Ruby said. She didn't want to tell Pa the reason.

Pa walked her to school anyway. On the way there, Ruby dawdled, considering what to try next. By the time they made the turn onto Warren Avenue,

Pa and Maude were ahead of her. *Good.* Ruby felt as low as a lizard's belly. *Maybe they will forget about me, and I can melt away like the spring snow.* She watched Maude trot toward the schoolyard to greet the other children, who were already scuffling to see who would be first to feed her a treat.

Then Ruby watched Pa. He reached the bottom of the school steps and tipped his hat at Miss Sternum. Miss Sternum seemed to have been waiting for him. Gloom descended around Ruby like a thick, gray fog. The school bell began to clang, and for a moment Ruby considered playing hooky. She could take Maude and spend the day in the hills by herself.

Maude seemed to have other ideas. She plunked down in her favorite spot, and Ruby didn't think she had a big enough lunch to convince her to leave. Ruby felt like she'd been squished by a moosesquatch. She walked slowly to class, plopped down in her seat, and stared at Agnes's perfectly twisted braid. She decided she would beat Agnes at every math question. And geography questions, too. If Ruby was going to be miserable, the rest of the world could be miserable, too.

"We have news about our hike up Mount Pisgah," Miss Logan began after the opening recitations. "We'll have Mr. Penn, a very distinguished geologist, joining us. He's an expert on the rock formations that have yielded Cripple Creek so much prosperity."

Agnes's hand shot up. "My uncle says the gold around here will never run out."

Miss Logan nodded and said, "Never is a long time, but we have been extremely fortunate with all of the abundance."

Lester Ward asked, "What does *abundance* mean?"

Agnes's hand shot up again. "It means we are blessed with plenty."

Ruby frowned. *Blessed with plenty.* She didn't want to feel happy about anything right now.

"And one more thing," Miss Logan said. "Miss Sternum has given permission for Maude to go along with us." She paused. "We'd like to treat our guest, Mr. Penn, to a ride up Mount Pisgah."

Ruby sprang to her feet and started to object to Maude's work assignment when a look from Miss Logan shriveled her. "Miss Sternum would not be pleased with your behavior right now, Ruby."

Ruby slumped back down in her seat, trying to decide how to tell Maude she'd be carrying a distinguished geologist to the top of Mount Pisgah.

* * *

After school Ruby and Maude raced down Bennett Avenue, looking for Amos. He was her last hope for getting some advice about flames, disaster, and Pa's lovesickness. Ruby breathed a sigh of relief when she saw him sitting outside Palace Drug.

"Almost finished." Amos made one last notch in the small model he was whittling and handed it to Ruby.

"It looks just like Maude!" Ruby turned the carved donkey over and over in her hands and studied every detail. She held it out to Maude, who sniffed at it and nickered with approval. "It's perfect." Ruby admired the way Amos had made tiny notches along the donkey's mane to make it look real.

Amos shrugged. "It helps pass the time." Ruby started to hand the figure back. "You keep it. I made it for you, and if you don't take it, I'll have to give it to my second best girlfriend." He winked at Ruby and stroked Maude's neck.

This reminded Ruby of why she'd come. "Have you ever had a real girlfriend?" she asked. "I mean one that was a person?"

Amos chuckled. "Lots of them. But they never did stick."

"Why not?" Ruby sat down next to Amos.

"Jealousy," Amos said. "I had more than one gal tell me if I didn't stop paying so much attention to my donkey, they'd up and leave. And that's what happened."

"You mean they thought you couldn't love them and Sylvia, too?"

"That's the way women are," Amos said. "If they sniff competition, they're going to hightail it somewhere else. It's jealousy, plain and simple."

Ruby turned the wood carving over in her hands, thinking. She needed a plan to make Miss Sternum jealous. But that meant Pa would have to have another girlfriend. Ever since Ma died, he hadn't been interested in anyone. Until now. Ruby's gloomy mood returned.

"You look like you could use some ice cream," Amos said, handing Ruby some pennies. "And Maude looks like she's about to starve."

Ruby glanced over at Maude licking the glass of the Palace Drug window. She put the carving in her pocket and went inside for ice cream. She was waiting for the penny licks when she heard Maude snort.

Ruby looked out through the glass. Maude trotted away from the window, turned and loped back, brayed, and trotted away again. Ruby grabbed the ice cream and started out. She wedged her foot into the door and peered out at the street. Amos had hobbled to the middle of the street and stood with his back to her, talking to a man on a gray horse.

Jake Hawker. Ruby froze. Maude pushed the door, nudging Ruby back inside. Juggling the penny licks, Ruby pressed her face against the glass, trying to get a better view. She pushed on the door again and wiggled past Maude. By the time she reached the boardwalk, Hawker had turned his gray mount and ridden off.

Amos hobbled back to the bench, shaking his head. "Durndest thing," he said. "Durndest thing."

Ruby tried to control the panic in her voice. "Do you know that man?"

Amos studied her before answering. "Now girl, you'd better let Maude have that ice cream before she goes off like a stick of dynamite."

Maude started to settle as Ruby held out a shallow glass to her. Lapping in the air, Maude's tongue followed Ruby as she plunked down on the bench next to Amos.

"Now tell me what in thunder is going on with all the braying and yelling and running around."

"That man on the gray horse. He's the one that upset Maude," Ruby said.

"Hawker?"

"You know him?" Ruby didn't think it was possible that Amos could be a friend with that—that thief.

Amos spat. "Know him. That scoundrel. He's more crooked than a pig's tail."

"But why were you talking to him?" Ruby's mind whirled. She couldn't get answers fast enough.

"Funniest thing. He never did say. Seems our conversation halted as soon as you poked your head through the door." Amos paused. "As a matter of fact, Maude started acting up as soon as she saw him. She didn't seem to like him at all."

Too nervous for ice cream, Ruby tipped the second penny lick so Maude could get to it.

"You don't look good with a wrinkly face," Amos said, interrupting Ruby's thoughts. "If you're not careful, you'll end up looking like them old folks up yonder in the Catholic Hospital."

Ruby tried to shake off her worries. She needed to tell Pa about seeing Jake Hawker. But he was too busy spinning around town with Miss Sternum stuck to him like a leg trap on the foot of a mountain lion. Ruby took the empty ice cream glasses inside and came back out. She started pacing back and forth in the street below the boardwalk. Maude followed, turning when she did and reversing to head back in the other direction.

Amos sighed with exasperation. "I never figured you to be related to a polecat."

Ruby stopped pacing and plopped down again. Maude stopped, too, staying close, with her ears alert. In a few minutes, Ruby had spilled out the whole story of Hawker and the candleholders and him being the reason she and Pa had come to live in Cripple Creek. She finished by telling about Pa and Miss Sternum and how her life would be practically ended if they got married.

"She'll send me to Madame Fleur's elocution class over at the Masonic Temple and make me learn to hold teacups properly." Ruby pinched her thumb and fingers together, keeping her pinky straight. She pretended to sip from an imaginary cup, making loud slurping sounds as she did.

Amos slapped a hand on one knee and let out a loud guffaw. "I'll be durned if you need help learning to drink tea. But you might work on quieting it down a little."

Ruby felt a little better having someone to talk to, but she wasn't any closer to figuring out what to do about things. She started to tell Amos about her visit to the fortune-teller—the flames and disaster, but when she looked over at him, he had an odd look on his face.

Snap! Amos clicked his fingers. Startled, Maude jerked her head up and swiveled her ears. "Don't know why I didn't think of it sooner. I think I seen your candleholders."

"Where?" Ruby became as alert as Maude.

"Little short fella with black hair, kinda long." Amos chopped with one hand near his neck. "He was walkin' around peddlin' a whole bundle of 'em. Didn't like the looks of him, neither," Amos continued. "He kept lookin' around like maybe he was gonna get snake bit if he wasn't careful."

The man that had been lingering around the

school! Now Ruby knew why the man that had been standing with him one day looked so familiar. It was that crook, Jake Hawker.

"I have to go," Ruby said. She grabbed Maude's lead rope and ran to the El Paso Livery to look for Pa. She flew through the front door and scanned the area near the forge.

"Are you looking for your pa?" a man wearing a leather apron asked.

"Is he here?"

"Just left," the man said. "Told me he was off to buy a little trinket of some kind. Must be sweet on someone." The man raised an eyebrow at Ruby.

Ruby's eyebrows lowered. She stamped out of the livery. "Come on, Maude. We need to make a plan."

Fourteen

Ruby had it all figured out. She'd tell Miss Sternum the most awful story about Pa so that Miss Sternum would drop him like a hot spoon. The plan bothered Ruby because she'd have to stretch the truth a little. Some people might call that a lie, but Pa had always said that telling a good story was a talent. *A God-given talent.* Isn't that what he had called it?

Another thing Pa often said was, "What's *best for us* and *what we want* are two different things." Ruby knew what was best for Pa. Or at least she thought she did. For sure she knew what was best for Ruby May Oliver—keeping Pa from hitching up with Miss Sternum.

On the morning of the Mount Pisgah hike, Ruby was ready to put her plan into action. She practiced her story as she walked with Maude past the Warren

Avenue School toward the Mount Pisgah Cemetery. "This had better work," Ruby told Maude. "If not, we're going to have to hit the trail on our own."

Ruby watched the other students arrive. Agnes Gribbell jumped from a fancy carriage and joined her friends near the cemetery entrance. A group of the younger children spotted Maude and ran to greet her. Maude made a throaty half-bray and trotted ahead to meet them.

When Ruby caught up, she glanced around for Miss Sternum. There she stood in a small group surrounding a short man smoking a pipe. Ruby decided it was Mr. Penn. He waved his arms and spouted like the volcano he was talking about. "A batholyth of molten rock." He pointed to Pikes Peak. "It's one of the oldest mountains in Colorado … pushed up millions of years ago."

Ruby waited for him to finish, wondering if she'd get a chance to tell Miss Sternum her story. Miss Sternum didn't look like she was going to leave Mr. Penn's side anytime soon. She appeared spellbound as he prattled on about granite uplifts and folds.

Ruby shifted from foot to foot and stared west at the summit of Mount Pisgah. It wasn't anything like the big peaks she and Pa had climbed. It fanned out evenly like a woman's skirt and had a big knob of rock on the top. Ruby didn't figure it would take long to climb. They'd be down by noon, just as Miss

Sternum had told them.

"Oh goodness," Miss Sternum snapped out of her trance and looked at her timepiece. "We'd better get started." She spotted Ruby. "Have you brought Maude?"

Ruby had forgotten that Miss Sternum had volunteered Maude to carry Mr. Penn up Mount Pisgah. Worse, she'd forgotten to tell Maude about it. It took a few minutes to coax her away from the children and their treats.

Miss Sternum smiled as Ruby approached. She turned to Mr. Penn. "This," she said, clasping her hands to her chest, "is your ride up Mount Pisgah."

Mr. Penn studied Maude. "That's quite kind of you, Miss Sternum, but I did not expect a special favor when I agreed to come."

Appearing a bit flustered, Miss Sternum said, "Our experts deserve the utmost courtesy."

"As do you." Mr. Penn made a sweep of his hand toward Maude's back. "I would like you to have my ride up the mountain."

Ruby looked over at Maude, trying to decide if this would be a good or a bad idea. If Maude decided to get contrary ...

Miss Sternum gushed. "You mustn't fuss over me."

"I insist." Bending slightly at the waist, Mr. Penn made another gesture toward Maude.

Just above Miss Sternum's collar, a patch of red began to grow, spreading up her neck and blooming like scarlet chrysanthemums on her cheeks.

"Well ..." Miss Sternum seemed undecided.

The children waiting for the hike started to scatter. Some had spread into the cemetery, jumping over the graves and playing tag. Another group, the ones who had been feeding Maude, started up Mount Pisgah on their own. They ran on ahead, seeming to care little that the adults had been left behind.

Ruby held Maude's lead, still weighing the possibilities of what she might coax Maude to do if Miss Sternum were the rider. Maude made the decision for everyone. She tipped her head back and brayed. After three loud bellows, she yanked the rope out of Ruby's hands and trotted after the runaway children, kicking up her heels in a playful way. The rope dragged on the ground behind her.

Ruby ran after Maude, hollering for her to hold up. But the farther she was from Miss Sternum, the more lighthearted Ruby felt. She began to skip and run not really caring if she caught Maude or not. "I'll race you," Ruby called to Lizzy as she passed the first group of children.

"Wait!" Lizzy dashed to catch up.

Ruby didn't wait. She ran until her sides ached. Stopping to catch her breath, she scanned the hillside below. Lizzy, with Maude at her heels, was not far behind. The other students and teachers were strung out in small groups, gradually making their way up the slope. Miss Sternum and Mr. Penn brought up the rear. Mr. Penn, nearly half a head shorter than Miss Sternum, bobbed along beside her with his arms flying every which way as he talked.

Ruby wanted to be first to the top. She started off again, jogging and walking until she was just below the crown. She scrambled up the rocky crest to a place where she had a full view in every direction. Breathing the thin air in quick gulps, she looked east toward Pikes Peak, which had snow still pocketed under the high ridges.

A long, wide valley stretched to the west, and beyond that layers and layers of mountains, their brown ridges showing as the winter snow melted. It reminded Ruby of her travels with Pa and the taste of water from a mountain glacier.

Ruby wanted the moment to last forever. Instead, the chatter of the hikers spoiled her solitude. Lizzy clambered to the top first and sat down next to Ruby. A few boys, who had raced the last twenty feet, were next. Maude stayed below, munching on a patch of mountain bromegrass.

"Pa's diggins is down there." Lizzy pointed.

Ruby looked at a long, low ridge that rose up beyond the cemetery to the south of Cripple Creek. One side of the hill gently sloped toward town, and the other dropped down into a long, curvy gulch. The hill was speckled with rock piles and wooden frames used for hoists where prospectors had staked claims.

"Pa thinks he's going to strike it rich," Lizzy continued. "And he owns this claim fair and square. I seen his papers."

Ruby smiled at Lizzy and watched Miss Sternum and Mr. Penn ascend the last few feet to a wide spot below the summit. After stopping to catch her breath, Miss Sternum called the group together for Mr. Penn's geology lecture. Ruby climbed down and scratched Maude's ears. She didn't want to hear about volcanoes and gold veins. During the talk, she daydreamed about what it would be like to camp by the little stream that wiggled through the wide valley to the west or to travel to the distant mountains.

"Are there any questions?" Miss Sternum asked after Mr. Penn had finished his talk.

Ruby wanted to ask if Miss Sternum had ever been camping. Had she slept out under the stars and seen the sun rise through the flap of a tent? Maude nudged Ruby's cheek. "You understand, don't you?" Ruby whispered. She stroked Maude again.

The snap of a pocket watch caused Ruby to look up. "Is it that time already?" Miss Sternum asked.

Mr. Penn slipped his watch back into vest pocket. "It's nearly noon."

Ruby sighed as she watched Miss Sternum and Mr. Penn lead the group down. Reluctantly she followed. The more Ruby thought about it, the more the idea of running away with Maude sounded good. She discarded her plan for telling Miss Sternum a story about Pa. It would be simpler just to leave.

"Just the two of us," Ruby said when she reached Maude. "We could go wherever we wanted. And sleep out under the stars again."

Without Pa. A lump formed in Ruby's throat. Traveling without Pa would be like having a fish to fry and no pan to cook it in. Ruby's mood sank lower with every step down the side of Mount Pisgah. She didn't think things could get much worse.

Ruby was wrong. Agnes Gribbell hiked over and blurted out, "I hear your pa's sweet on Miss Sternum."

Ruby shrugged. It wasn't any of Agnes's business.

"Mr. Penn's a single man, too, you know. I bet your pa's no match for him."

Ruby bristled. "My pa's a match for just about anyone." Even though Ruby didn't want Pa to be sweet on Miss Sternum, she didn't like anyone saying he wasn't good enough. Especially Agnes.

"Miss Sternum's had plenty of suitors," Agnes said. "She's had chances to marry, but Mother says she'll die an old maid."

Ruby didn't care if Miss Sternum died an old maid. She just didn't want her to die as her ma. She looked over her shoulder to make sure Maude was still following along.

"One man who was courting her died of pneumonia," Agnes continued. "After that, she took sweet on a miner. He was blown to bits, and they had to bury him in pieces."

Ruby started to get a tight and uncomfortable feeling in her chest.

"The last man was a gambler who couldn't pay his debts, so they ran him out of town," Agnes finished.

"All of Miss Sternum's suitors have had bad luck?" Ruby asked. Maude trotted by, keeping a few paces ahead of the girls.

Agnes nodded. "Mother says misfortune follows Miss Sternum's suitors like metal to a magnet."

Misfortune. Ruby's heart thudded as her thoughts traveled to the candlelit room above Slusher's Grocery. A single word from Madam Estelle's palm reading echoed in Ruby's mind. *Disaster.*

Fifteen

"What's wrong with your donkey?" Agnes pointed.

Ruby looked at Maude. She stood frozen with her ears pointed forward as straight as twin twigs. Not one muscle twitched. Maude focused on something in the distance, down the slope of Mount Pisgah toward the center of Cripple Creek. Ruby sidled up next to Maude and listened. Concentrating hard, she could hear the mockingbird alarm from the Gold King Mine. The steam whistle echoed long and persistent, like a hungry baby wailing for food.

Then Ruby saw it—a plume of smoke, rising from the center of town. Next, yellow flames shot up, and in what seemed like seconds, a black cloud formed.

"Fire!" someone down the slope shouted. The children were pointing and calling back and forth to each other. Teachers tried to calm them, but some were already crying, and a few were bolting toward the cemetery where their hike had started.

"Pa!" Ruby started to run. A wave of terror flooded through her as she dashed past small groups of panicked students.

"Wait!" Lizzy cried. "Wait for us!" Lizzy led Maude at a trot, trying to catch up with Ruby.

Ruby stopped long enough to swing Lizzy up on Maude's back and set out again. Behind her, Maude clomped and bumped down the hill. "You're going too fa-a-a-st!" Lizzy gripped Maude's mane.

As they neared the cemetery, the puffs of smoke that had seemed small from a distance, hovered like thick clouds over the town. Flames crackled, and fire bells clanged.

Ruby stopped at the cemetery entrance. *Where was Pa?* Fine bits of debris fell from the sky. Her lungs burned, and her eyes stung. The terror that had filled her when she first saw the fire returned. *Where was Pa?* Wagons, carts, and buggies clattered past, piled high with tables, chairs, clothing, anything of value that might burn.

"Turn around. Go back!" a man shouted from one of the wagons. "The whole town's about to blow!"

"Head to the reservoir," someone else yelled.

Ruby glanced at the hill on the north side toward the reservoir. Houses there were untouched. The area to the south, where Ruby and Lizzy lived, was well away from the fire.

"I want my ma." Lizzy slid off Maude's back and started to cry.

An explosion shook the ground, and fresh flames leapt up. Lizzy covered her ears, sobbing loudly. Maude joined her, braying and bellowing. She trotted away from the direction of the fire, then returned, stamping and swinging her head as if calling the girls away from danger.

Ruby barely noticed. One horror-filled thought filled her mind. *Pa. Where would he be? How close was the fire to the livery?*

Miss Sternum, breathless and disheveled, caught up with Ruby. "Children, we *must* stay together." Two young girls with wide, frightened eyes gripped Miss Sternum's skirt.

"I wanna go home," Lizzy cried. She took two steps before Mr. Penn grabbed her arm and pulled her back into the group.

Ruby's terror grew. *Pa! I've got to find him!*

Another explosion, followed by a crack and the sound of splitting wood sent Lizzy and the younger children into wails of panic. More wagons rattled by and then hoofbeats drummed the ground as a string of animals raced past them.

Goldie and Lightning! Ruby recognized the two horses from the livery running amid the stampede of bays, blacks, and roans. Some were saddled, and some trailed halters and half-fastened tack.

The livery! Ruby bolted like one of the half-saddled horses.

"Miss Oliver!" Miss Sternum shouted after her. "Come back here this instant." The words drifted upward and disappeared like the smoke from the fire. *Pa!*

Ruby reached the edge of town and raced for the livery. Sparks and cinders rained down from the burning buildings to the east on Bennett Avenue. Ruby ripped a piece of cloth from the hem of her dress and tied it over her mouth and nose. Tears stung her eyes.

"Stay back," a man covered with soot hollered as he hurried down Bennett with a box of uncharged dynamite.

Ruby turned west toward the livery. When she got there, the doors hung open. "Pa! Pa!" The forge was abandoned, and the horse stalls were empty.

Something behind Ruby yowled. She spun around to see the wide eyes and arched back of a frightened yellow cat. When she reached for it, the cat hissed and backed away, then turned and ran.

"Pa!" Ruby yelled again. She dunked her

face cloth into the water tank near the forge and rewrapped it over her nose and mouth before darting back outside.

The fire was about two blocks away, beyond Palace Drug. Ruby started in that direction, hoping Pa would be there helping. A cart filled with letters from the post office rattled past, and two men jostled a sofa out the door of the Palace Hotel into an empty wagon. A man shouted to the driver, "I'll pay you ten dollars if you'll come back for my goods."

Two men passed by, rolling a whiskey keg away from the fire. They grinned back over their shoulders as someone shouted angrily at them. Across Bennett Avenue, the soda jerk from Palace Drug stood outside, still wearing his apron. He clutched a rifle to his chest. He shouted at two firefighters, "No one's going to use dynamite in here to stop the fire."

Another loud explosion destroyed a building at the boundary of the fire. Ashes and embers flew. A soot-covered man ran toward the Palace Hotel. He jumped onto the seat of a wagon ready for loading and shouted, "I need this rig!" He snapped the lines and drove off.

"Pa!" Ruby was sure it was Pa. The man didn't look back but drove east on Bennett into the thickest part of the smoke.

Ruby followed, hurrying past a fireman pointing a hose at one of the burning buildings. The fireman breathed through a sponge tied with twine over his nose and mouth. Ruby quickly wet her face cloth with the spray from a dripping hydrant. The spray suddenly stopped. "There's no more water!" The fireman shouted. His hose sagged limply.

Another man yelled at Ruby. "Get out of here!"

With stinging eyes, Ruby ran into the smoke, searching for the wagon she'd seen. Flames shot from the roof of the National Hotel bright enough for her to make out the shape of the wagon bed. Someone yelled, "It's coming down!" Men scattered, hunching over and running to escape the falling debris. The building crumpled.

"Pa!" Ruby shouted.

A man grabbed her by the arm and threw her out of the way as a window frame crashed at her feet. Another pair of hands dragged her down the street away from the collapsing buildings. She was thrown into a carriage filled with clothing from the Weinberg Store. The driver snapped the lines and the cart bumped away from the fire. Ruby stared back into the smoke and destruction. Her stomach twisted into a knot. *What had happened to Pa?*

Once out of danger, the horse and carriage turned north and climbed the hill to the reservoir. The driver halted next to bags of mail and post office furniture. "Special delivery," the driver said. The guard watching over the pile helped Ruby down.

All around her, people stood in groups by heaps of household belongings, staring gloomily down the hill at the ruin. The tears that Ruby had been holding back spilled out.

Mr. Penn bustled over, scribbling names in a small notebook. Miss Sternum followed him. "Oh thank goodness." Miss Sternum wrung her hands with worry. "You should never have run off like that!"

Ruby wiped away her tears with her fist. She looked past Miss Sternum to where Lizzy sat hunched over, gazing down the hill at the fire, her knees pulled up to her chest. Ruby walked over and dropped down beside her. "My ma's probably wondering where I am," Lizzy sniffled.

Ruby sighed. The fire seemed to be dying. On the east end of Bennett, the Midland Terminal still stood, but a large, smoldering hole gaped nearby where the buildings on Bennett and Myers had been. The dark, ashy area stretched up the hill below them where the spire from the Methodist Church stood looking like a spiked island surrounded by a blackened sea.

"I'm going to be in trouble," Lizzy continued to worry. "Ma told me to come right home after the hike to help her pluck chickens."

Miss Sternum stood guard over her flock, releasing the children one by one to their parents as they arrived. Mrs. Gribbell pulled up in her carriage, appearing flustered and out of sorts. She smiled with relief as Agnes climbed in. Mr. Penn made a checkmark in his book.

"Nobody's going to come for me," Lizzy continued to sulk. "We don't got no carriage."

The sun glowed orange in the smoke-filled sky as it sank slowly down behind Mount Pisgah. Ruby's stomach ached. All around the reservoir, people settled down near their small piles of household goods. "All gone. Everything gone," she heard one woman sob.

Before the sun completely disappeared, people from the nearby communities of Victor and Goldfield began to arrive with food and offers of shelter. Ruby stared at the smoking ruins. *Where was Pa?* She imagined the worst.

"You better get home quick." Ruby glanced up to see Lizzy's brother, Franky, running toward them. "I've been around this mud puddle twice looking for you."

Lizzy popped up and trotted after her brother. "I'm going now, Miss Sternum." She waved, and Ruby watched them disappear.

A few more carriages and wagons arrived to deliver goods and to haul the townspeople to homes and shelters. People bundled up their belongings or left them stacked in the care of those waiting for news of family or friends. Except for a few fiery flare-ups, the flames dwindled, and the smoke cloud began to thin.

Ruby stared into the gloom, thinking of the last time she'd seen Pa. Images of the National Hotel collapsing haunted her. Over and over, the building collapsed in her mind. Timbers cracked, and cinders rained down. Ruby spiraled down into a deeper pit of worry. What would she do if she lost Pa?

Sixteen

"We'd better go now." Miss Sternum interrupted Ruby's thoughts.

"Go where?" Ruby looked up.

"It's best you stay with me until we're able to find your father."

"I'll just wait here a little longer," Ruby said. "If Pa doesn't show up after a while, I'll go home and wait for him there."

"Young lady," Miss Sternum said firmly. "We are going." Ruby was too tired to argue. She dragged herself up, realizing she was the only child from school whose family had not come.

Mr. Penn walked over, still carrying his notebook. "May I escort you home?" he asked.

"No thank you," Miss Sternum said. "It's not far, and I shall have Ruby as company."

Ruby walked in silence to Miss Sternum's house on the east side of Golden Avenue. Every few steps, Ruby looked over her shoulder. *Still no Pa.* Slowly she followed Miss Sternum up the walkway to a neatly painted two-story house. Miss Sternum opened the door and lit the lamp on a small, round table in the hallway.

"Well ..." Miss Sternum's sigh nearly blew out the flame as she replaced the decorative chimney on the lamp. "I'll fix a little something to eat and make sure the guest room is in order." She removed her wrap and hung it on the coat stand next to the door.

Ruby glanced beyond the entryway into the parlor, where a green upholstered chair perched like an animal on clawed wooden feet. A matching sofa stretched along one wall in front of a window with lacey white curtains. She felt Miss Sternum's gaze on the top of her head. It traveled down her body to her soot-covered boots, lingering on the hem of Ruby's dress where the strip of cloth had been torn off. Miss Sternum sighed again. "I suppose, first, a bath is in order."

Ruby removed her blackened boots and left them by the door. Tiptoeing, she followed Miss Sternum up a narrow flight of steps, making sure she didn't touch the polished banister that reflected the light from the lamp.

At the top of the stairs, she followed Miss Sternum down a narrow hallway to the room at the end. Ruby stared, wide-eyed. The large water closet had a tub, a toilet, and a basin. Centered along one wall, a pot-bellied stove stood ready to be lighted.

"Get undressed," Miss Sternum said matter-of-factly. "I'll get this stove going so you can have some hot water."

Ruby shifted from foot to foot, not wanting to undress in front of Miss Sternum. She thought about the time when she and Pa had pitched their tent next to a dead cottonwood tree, sky showing between the bare branches. Ruby, only five at the time, had asked Pa, "What happened to that tree's clothes?"

Pa had laughed and patted Ruby's head. "Shhhh. You don't want that tree to die of embarrassment."

Ruby had been too young to get the joke, but if things really did die of embarrassment, she'd be gasping her last breath about now.

"Oh fiddlesticks." Miss Sternum dropped a matchstick onto the kindling in the pot-bellied stove. It fizzled and went out.

"Let me try," Ruby said. "I'm good at building fires."

Miss Sternum gave her a doubtful look. "Surely your father would not allow you."

Ruby stifled a snort. It had always been her job to start the campfire while Pa staked the tent. She'd gotten so she could lay the kindling and get a blaze going with only one match. Ruby had learned to carry a ball of pine pitch so she could build a fire, even in the rain. Pa called her the fire magician.

"I can heat my own bath water, too," Ruby said.

Miss Sternum straightened up and brushed her skirt. After a long exhale, she handed the match safe to Ruby. "Let me know if you need more."

"I won't," Ruby assured her. Miss Sternum left and closed the door behind her.

A minute later, Ruby had the fire roaring. It brought back the terror of the smoke-filled afternoon. She closed the stove door and walked to a small window overlooking the street. The house was high enough to view the burned section of town. A smoky haze still hung in the air, and her fear about Pa hovered with it.

Trying not to worry, Ruby poured hot water into the tub, mixing it with cold to the right temperature. She sank down in the bath, adding a dab of Miss Sternum's bath oil to the water. She soaked until the water lost its heat, then, remembering to scrub, she finished up.

The water looked like mud. The rest of the dirt ended up on the white towel Miss Sternum had left for her. Ruby slipped on her underclothes and peeked out the door. Miss Sternum appeared carrying a clean nightgown.

"Pa wouldn't want me taking clothes from a stranger."

Miss Sternum frowned and looked past Ruby at the dirty towel, which had been tossed on the floor. Ruby hurried to hang it up. Bundling her remaining clothes, she followed Miss Sternum to a bedroom next to the water closet. The quilt had been turned down on the bed, and two puffy pillows perched on the stiffly starched sheets.

"I've brought you dinner," Miss Sternum said, pointing to the plate on a small table next to the bed. "I'll lay this here in case you change your mind." She placed the nightgown on a chest of drawers next to a window. "I imagine you're tired."

Ruby thought Miss Sternum was the one who looked tired. Underneath her glasses, dark circles swelled under her eyes. "I'll be leaving early," Ruby said. "I need to find my pa."

"Yes, of course. We're both worried." Miss Sternum rubbed the back of her neck.

"You don't understand," Ruby said. "He's *my* pa." The word *my* shot out forcefully.

Miss Sternum stiffened. "We'll find him in the morning."

The morning! Ruby's stomach twisted into a knot.

"I'll be downstairs if you need me," Miss Sternum said, pulling the door closed. The floorboards in the hallway creaked loudly as Miss Sternum walked away.

After eating her dinner, Ruby began to pace. She circled past the bed, the window, the bureau, the closed door, and back again. After several rounds, she flopped onto the bed, sinking into one of the fluffed-up pillows. *What if Pa had gone home and was looking for her? How would he know where to find her?*

Ruby had never spent a night alone. She'd always had Pa or Maude with her. *Maude!* Ruby sprang up. *Where was Maude?* Ruby flung open the window and leaned out, looking left and right down the street. She couldn't remember the last time she'd seen Maude. They'd been at the cemetery with all of the wagons and horses galloping past.

Ruby tried to reassure herself. Probably Maude had found her way home. Ruby made another circle of the room. She imagined Maude standing outside their cabin waiting for her. Hungry and waiting. Alone and hungry and waiting.

This made Ruby feel worse. She should have thought about Maude sooner. She should never have left her. The past few hours had been an unending nightmare of terror. Still, how could she have forgotten Maude?

Ruby considered what to do. Going out the front door would be impossible. The floorboards in the hall made too much noise. And if she got caught, Miss Sternum would probably stand guard over her for the rest of the night.

Ruby leaned out the bedroom window again. Light from a downstairs window cast a glow on the ground below. Too far to jump. She leaned out a little farther. The gabled roof that covered the front entrance to the house was only a few feet away. If she could balance herself on the frame of the downstairs window and stretch over to it, she could slide down one of the pillars holding up the roof and get to the ground.

Ruby dressed quickly and looked around the room for something she could rig up to help her cross the space between the window and the gabled roof. She spotted the nightgown Miss Sternum had brought for her. Ruby tied the arms of the nightgown to one of the upright bedposts and tested it for strength. She peered out again, measuring the distance in her mind.

The light downstairs flickered and faded, leaving the outside of the house reflected in moonlight. Ruby heard Miss Sternum's footsteps on the stairs. She turned off her own lamp and waited. The floorboards of the hall squeaked and stopped outside Ruby's door. After a long pause, the floorboards creaked again, and a door closed with a click.

Ruby had been holding her breath. She exhaled,

letting the jitters squirm down her body and wiggle out her toes. A few seconds later, she climbed over the windowsill and grasped the nightgown, using it as an anchor as she lowered herself down to the frame of the window below. In her stocking feet, she carefully inched across the thin ledge of the window frame.

Only one long step. Ruby took a deep breath, stretched, and ... riiiipppp! The shoulder seam of the nightgown split. Ruby clutched and wobbled as a few more threads popped. Frantic, Ruby released the nightgown and lunged. She belly flopped onto the roof, digging in with fingernails and toes to keep from sliding off.

Heart pounding, Ruby rolled over and sat up. She crawled to the edge of the roof and slipped over the lip, wrapping her arms and legs around the wooden pillar. She shimmied down and landed with a soft thud. Glancing at her snagged and torn stockings, Ruby thought about going back inside for her boots, but decided against it. No telling what Miss Sternum would do if she got caught now.

Miss Sternum. Guilt gnawed at Ruby as she tiptoed across the yard. Then she thought about Maude and Pa. She struck out, planning to follow the railroad tracks behind the terminal and turn back to the west once she'd cleared the burned area of town.

Ruby slowed as she neared the east end of Bennett. Men still worked, dousing small fires and sifting through the rubble. Shovels clanked and freight wagons creaked between the fallen buildings as the cleanup began. Ruby hesitated. One of those men could be Pa or someone who knew him.

"You there. Stop!" A gunshot rang out, and Ruby froze, throwing her arms up over her head. A man strode from the shadows, pointing a long pistol. "What are you doing out here this time of night?"

Ruby swallowed, her throat dry from the thick ash that filled the air. "Going home," she rasped.

The man barked, "You shouldn't be out here by yourself."

Ruby still held her hands up, wondering why the man had stopped her. Then she noticed a badge pinned to the front of his shirt. The badge was ragged around the edges and not quite as shiny as the other badges she'd seen deputies wearing.

"There are looters and thieves all over the place," the man said gruffly. "You sure you're not hiding anything?" He leaned forward and squinted at her suspiciously.

"No sir," Ruby said. "I live over there." She pointed south toward the unburned section of town.

The man motioned with his gun. "Go on, then. And don't let me see you around here again."

Ruby ran until her lungs hurt, and then she slowed to a walk. As she approached the cabin, she prayed for a glimmer of light in the window. She prayed that Maude would be standing by the door or that Pa would be inside.

Nothing moved. Moonlight reflected off the cold stovepipe, and not one wisp of smoke stirred. *Maude would have heard me by now, would have come trotting over.*

Rounding the corner of the house, Ruby stared at the empty place next to the door where Maude slept. "Maude!" She walked around the house and checked the shed, just to be sure.

It was dark and deathly quiet when Ruby entered the cabin. As she struck a match, the light flickered on Pa's empty cot. Ruby flopped on her bed and closed her eyes, planning to rest a few minutes and then start looking again. *If the hospitals had burned, where would they take the people who were hurt?*

Ruby shook off the thought. Maybe both Pa and Maude had gone looking for her, and both of them would be home soon. She reached to the little shelf next to her bed where she kept the carving of Maude that Amos had given her. Clutching it tightly, she drifted off.

The next thing Ruby knew, sunlight crept in through the east window. Quietly, the door opened and closed. "Pa!" Ruby sprang up and flew across the room, flinging her arms around his middle and clutching him tightly.

"Now there. If you keep squeezing me like that, you're going to turn me into a licorice stick." He hugged Ruby back.

Ruby wiped her eyes. "I f-f-followed you into the fire. I tried to find you." She sniffled, trying not to explode into tears. "And then ..." Ruby thought about Lizzy and Maude and Miss Sternum. She hesitated before telling the part of the story where she climbed out of Miss Sternum's window.

A knock at the door saved her the trouble. Pa opened it. There stood Miss Sternum, holding Ruby's filthy boots as if they might bite her. Ruby swallowed and stepped backward. Miss Sternum's voice sounded strained. "I believe these belong to Ruby."

Pa took the boots and invited Miss Sternum in. "I've just gotten home myself."

It was then Ruby noticed the star-shaped badge pinned to Pa's shirt. It had the same ragged tin edges as the badge she'd seen on the man that had stopped her along the tracks. A deputy. Pa had been made a deputy.

"There was so much looting last night," Pa explained. "They needed men to keep the saloons closed and guard the valuables that weren't burned up."

"Well, I shouldn't detain you," Miss Sternum said. "Perhaps your daughter will give you an explanation of her behavior last night."

Ruby's heart sank as Pa looked one direction and then the other. "I was worried about you, and ..." she began. Tears threatened to spill out again.

"Please come in," Pa said, removing his hat and combing his fingers through his smoky hair. He glanced sideways at Ruby, raising one eyebrow. Ruby knew this look well.

"No, thank you," Miss Sternum said. "I believe another time would be better."

"Allow me to escort you home."

"I have my conveyance." She paused. "And in spite of the fire, the Methodist Church still stands. I do not plan to miss Sunday services." Without another word, Miss Sternum spun around, climbed onto her bicycle, and pedaled away.

Pa stood in the doorway, watching Miss Sternum leave. When he came back in, he was still holding Ruby's boots. He looked from the boots to Ruby and waited.

"Pa, I was scared. I thought you'd been burned up, too." The flood of tears that Ruby had been holding back gushed out. She told him about the hike, following him into the fire, going to Miss Sternum's house, her escape out the window. She told him everything, and when she told him about

Maude, tears exploded again. She hiccuped through the story, ending with a final loud sob. "How will we ever find her?"

Pa pulled Ruby toward him again, hugging her to his tear-drenched shirt. "She'll come back," Pa said. "After all the excitement dies down, she'll trot right into the yard."

Pa was usually right. Ruby sagged a little with relief and then noticed his red, tired eyes. "Pa, you haven't had any sleep."

"I don't reckon you've had much either." He lifted her and carried her to bed as if she were a small child again. He tucked her in and patted her. "You know there are still some things we need to talk about."

"Hmmmm …" Ruby was already drifting off.

"After you've had a little more sleep, you're going to have to apologize to Miss Sternum for your behavior."

Ruby's eyes flicked open. "But Pa …"

"Not now," Pa said. "We'll talk about it after I've had a little shut-eye."

A few minutes later, Ruby heard Pa snoring. Ruby lay awake, thinking about Maude. Her hand found the wooden carving near her pillow. She studied it in the dim light, fingering the carefully whittled ears and stroking the carved donkey's spine.

Ruby ached for the real Maude. It wasn't like her

to disappear. She always found a way to get home. Always. Even the time Pa left Maude in the livery in Durango. She'd busted out and found them at the hotel.

Ruby tossed and turned. After a long while of trying to sleep, she flicked the blankets aside and tiptoed to the door to peek out. No sign of Maude. She pulled on her boots, scribbled a note to Pa, and left the cabin.

Seventeen

The bitter smell of smoke hung in the air as Ruby neared the burned section of town. People milled about in the early dawn, sifting through the burnt remains with shovels and sticks. In the daylight, it was easy to see where the fire had stopped. Ruby glanced up the hill toward the Methodist Church and the blackened buildings surrounding it. She imagined Miss Sternum preparing for the early morning service.

Miss Sternum. Doubt and confusion gnawed at Ruby. She knew she'd behaved poorly. It didn't make her feel very good, but the idea of apologizing made her feel even worse. If only she had Maude to talk to.

Ruby skirted the collapsed buildings on Myers and turned west on Bennett toward the El Paso Livery. She'd start looking there. Maybe Maude had showed up with some of the other runaways and been locked up by mistake.

A small figure dashed past. "Lizzy!"

Lizzy halted. Her eyes grew round, and her cheeks reddened. She clung to a burlap bag that was stuffed full and slung over one shoulder.

"What are you doing?" Ruby asked.

Lizzy lowered the bag. "Pa told me to run down here and fill this bag with anything I could get my hands on."

"Your pa wanted you to come down here and steal?" Ruby asked.

Lizzy stared at her shoes, her shoulders sagging. "Pa said nobody would notice if a few things was missing."

Ruby couldn't believe anything of value would have survived the fire, and she couldn't believe that Lizzy's pa had sent her out looting. "Did you find anything?"

Lizzy's eyes brightened. "You're never going to believe it." She opened the bag and began pulling out a long piece of red velvet cloth. It made a small mountain on the ground at her feet.

Ruby didn't speak. She stared at the pile of damp, charred fabric. She couldn't imagine what Lizzy wanted with it. "It's from the stage where they do all those fancy shows. Maybe Ma can wash it up and sew me a new dress."

Ruby had to agree with Lizzy's pa. No one would miss *that.* "What else do you have?"

Lizzy dove to the bottom of the bag and came back up with a smoke-blackened spittoon. She rubbed a little piece of it with her sleeve, and the brass shined through. "It's for my pa," Lizzy said. She held it up.

"Did that come from the concert hall, too?"

Lizzy beamed. "Do you want to hold it?"

Ruby shuddered, thinking about all the men who had spat tobacco juice into it. She wasn't about to touch it. "What's your pa going to do if the sheriff comes around?"

"I guess he'll hide it in the cellar with his hooch."

There were a few other odds and ends in the bag: a chipped dinner plate, two blackened spoons, and an ink bottle with a burned cork. "I don't think you should come back," Ruby said. "They're arresting looters."

Lizzy frowned. "Pa says I should grab everything I can, and Ma says it's the only chance we have of getting rich in Cripple Creek."

Ruby sighed and helped Lizzy put the items back in her bag. "Have you seen Maude?"

Lizzy blinked vacantly as she closed up the burlap. "Maude's gone?"

"She didn't come home after the fire," Ruby said, trying to keep the wobbles out of her voice. "I'm

148

looking for her."

"I'll help you," Lizzy said.

"You'd better take that sack home first," Ruby said. "I'm going to check the livery, then head up to the cemetery to see if I can find her tracks."

Lizzy hoisted the bag and started off at a trot. "I'll be there as soon as I can."

When Lizzy arrived at the cemetery, Ruby was pacing back and forth, studying the hoofprints. "They're all mixed up," she said. "Horse tracks and buggy tracks and boot tracks." She remembered the stampede. Finding Maude's tracks would be like separating sugar from salt.

"We could just follow the big trail," Lizzy suggested. "And maybe the tracks will thin out after a while."

Ruby considered this. "Maude always figures out a way to find me," she worried out loud.

"Maybe she's on her way home."

Ruby shook her head. "She would have been there before now."

After a little more thought, Ruby decided that following the tracks of the big herd was the best idea. She started off with Lizzy at her side. They followed the broken ground around the cemetery and up Signal Hill, weaving around mine shafts and dry holes. As the hoofprints began to drop down Long Hungry Gulch, the trees and brush crowded together, and the tracks became harder and harder to see.

Ruby wiped sweat from her face with the back of her sleeve. "This is what Pa would call bushwhacking country. If they went down there, we'll never find them."

"My pa's mine shaft is not too far from here," Lizzy said. "Maybe we can go ask him."

"Your pa's at the claim right now?" Ruby had figured he would be in town looting.

"He's got a meetin'," Lizzy said. "Someone's going to grubstake his claim, so he'll have enough money to keep working."

Ruby decided not to ask, but as they neared the claim, loud singing rose from a small mine shaft framed at the top by wood bracings. Attached to the wood frame was a small hand pulley to haul buckets of rock in and out of the hole.

Ruby followed Lizzy over to the opening and peered down. A rickety ladder leaned against the wall, stopping about twenty feet below where a tunnel angled off to one side. Candlelight flickered from the tunnel.

"Pa?" Lizzy called down.

The singing stopped abruptly. "Who'sh calling my name?" The words were slurred and unclear.

"It's Lizzy. And my friend, Ruby Oliver."

"Is that the girl with the donkey?"

"It's me," Ruby called.

A head appeared, and the ladder creaked as Joe McAvery climbed out of the shaft. He squinted for a minute, letting his eyes adjust to the light. "Did you find me any liquor in town?" He eyed Lizzy expectantly.

Lizzy shook her head. "Ma said she'd skin me alive if I brought back hooch. We're out here looking for Maude."

Lizzy's pa teetered over the hole, then wobbled forward just in time to catch himself. "The donkey?"

Lizzy nodded. "The tracks came up this way from the cemetery."

Joe scratched his beard then slapped the pocket of his shirt and looked around uneasily. "Where'd those papers go?" He scanned the ground around the opening to his pit. "Doggone it. You see anybody around here when you came up?"

Ruby stared. "No sir. We've been looking for donkey tracks."

Joe McAvery scuffed up the dirt around his feet then circled the opening to his mine, looking closely at the soil. He stopped where a wooden stake marked one of the boundaries of his claim. Ruby followed his gaze. The ground near the stake had been stirred to dust, as if something had been tied there. Beyond that the tracks of a single horse led away from the spot.

As if Lizzy had the same thought as Ruby, she asked, "Pa, was that man you talked about here?"

"Doggone it! Doggone it!" Joe McAvery cursed. "I'm never going to drink again for as long as I live." He crossed his heart with two long sweeps of his hand, nearly losing his balance on the second swipe.

Ruby shifted nervously. She wanted to get back to finding Maude, but Lizzy's pa was so riled up she didn't know what to do. "Pardon me, Mr. McAvery. If you've seen any of the animals that escaped the fire, we'd sure appreciate knowing about it."

McAvery shook his head and felt his empty pocket again. "Reckon they've gone with my papers. Schlick as a whistle. Some thief on a gray horse rode off with them." Lizzy's pa stumbled and caught himself. "Left thish poor fool hangin' out to dry."

"Jake Hawker?" Ruby yelped. "He's the man that stole your papers?" Her heart thumped loudly. "He was here? The man with the gray horse was here?"

"The sh-scoundrel," he muttered. "If he can figure out a way to get something that don't belong to him, he's gonna do it." McAvery slumped down on the rock pile next to his claim and buried his face in his hands. "Hawker sweet-talked me with a bottle of whisshkey, and I signed away the whole goldurned claim."

Ruby wasn't listening. She had to find Maude! *If that rotten Hawker had found her first ...* "Lizzy, we have to get going."

Lizzy's eyes filled with tears. "I can't leave Pa. There's no telling what he'll do."

Ruby understood. She knew that no matter what happened, she'd still love her own pa the same as Lizzy loved hers. Even if Pa decided to marry Miss Sternum. Ruby swallowed hard. She didn't want to think about Miss Sternum right now. She tried to shake off the image of the school principal standing in their doorway, holding her dirty boots.

As Lizzy continued to sniffle, Ruby heard a familiar sound in the distance. It was a faint, but persistent, braying. She was sure it was braying. "Lizzy," she said urgently. "Do you hear anything?"

Lizzy wiped away a tear with the sleeve of her blouse. She turned and looked out across the dry grass on the ridge, down toward Long Hungry Creek. She shook her head.

"There it is again!" Ruby leaned forward, straining to hear.

Lizzy wrinkled her face into a frown of concentration. She started to shake her head, then, "I hear it. I think I hear Maude!"

Both girls started running toward the sound. They reached the place where they'd last seen the tracks drop down into Long Hungry Gulch, and they stopped to listen.

Ruby studied the tracks, looking for signs of Maude. Instead, the curved shape of a fresh horse track was pressed into the ground on top of the others. The tracks dropped down into the gulch until the thick brush closed around them like a curtain. A sense of dread slithered down Ruby's spine.

"I don't think we should go any farther," Lizzy said. "I'm scared. And I shouldn't have left my pa."

Ruby studied the horse tracks. She was filled with indecision and almost ready to turn back when she heard the braying again. This time there wasn't any doubt. The sound drifted on the breeze from somewhere down Long Hungry Gulch. "It's Maude. We've got to go get her!"

Lizzy pleaded, "I've got to go take care of my pa."

For a moment, the braying stopped, then started again. It seemed weaker, like the bawling of an unhappy child hoarse from too much crying. Ruby ran, weaving her way through the maze of bushes, boulders, and trees. *Maude, I'm coming!*

Eighteen

At first Ruby could only pick out the fresh trail of a horse. But as she continued down the draw, broken branches through the brush marked a trail where a large group of hoofed animals had passed. The tracks looked as if the animals had been driven—as if someone was pushing them down the gulch.

Ruby wound her way down, avoiding areas where the bushes were too thick to go through and crossing open areas near the narrow creek where the bottom of the gully widened. There the tracks were easy to see. As Ruby descended, the gully deepened, making it harder for the sunlight to reach the brushy bottom.

After about a mile, Ruby stopped to catch her breath. She smelled smoke, and heard the clink of an enamel cup and men's voices drifting toward her. Ruby crept slowly ahead, tiptoeing to a place where the trail disappeared into a thick tangle of wild roses. She dropped to her belly and elbowed forward, hoping for a better view.

Beyond the brush, the gulch opened into a small flat area where a temporary pen had been built using rope and fallen trees. Maude stood inside the pen, tethered to a post. Behind her, tied nose to tail, were four other donkeys.

Ruby's heart skipped a beat. Then she heard the voices again. Not more than twenty feet away, two men sat with their backs to her, drinking a noontime cup of coffee. Two saddled horses stood nearby, swishing their tails idly. One of the horses was gray.

"I've already got the donkeys sold." Ruby recognized Hawker's voice. "I'll deliver them and catch up with you down at the abandoned homestead."

The other man put down his enamel cup. "I'll drive the horses into the corral and wait for you."

Hawker nodded, and then with a chuckle, he pulled some folded papers from the inside pocket of his jacket. "You'll never believe what I got that old drunk to do." He tapped the documents. "He signed over his claim to me. Probably just now getting sober enough to realize what happened."

The other man laughed and stood up. "Makes me no difference who you're cheating on the side. As long as I get my share of the livestock deals." The man walked a few feet and returned with a pot full of water to douse the fire. "And my cut for selling those candleholders." Ruby tensed as she recognized the man with the scraggly black hair.

"You sure no one can trace where these donkeys came from?" The fire hissed as the shorter man doused it. "We could take them with us and sell them with the horses."

Hawker snorted. "With that fire last night, no one's going to notice a few burros trailing up toward the mines. Once they're down underground, no one will know the difference."

Ruby tried to control the thumping in her chest, afraid her heart would jump right out. She wiggled until she could see the donkeys better. Maude's whole body sagged, and her ears drooped. *Maude.* Ruby sent a thought her way. One ear twitched, then wilted again. *Oh Maude.*

Ruby studied the distance she would have to cover to get to the pen. She could stay behind the bushes until she got closer. After that, she'd have to make a dash for it. If only Hawker were distracted for a few more minutes, she could get there, untie Maude, and ... then what?

The two men gathered up the reins to their horses. The short man walked to the lower end of the makeshift corral where the horses were roped off into a small group.

Maude started to bray. "Darn that donkey." Hawker hollered to his partner. "She's getting to be more trouble than she's worth." Hawker led his horse around the pen toward Ruby. He stopped right next to her hiding place, so close that Ruby could make out the stitching on his boots.

The scraggly-haired man yelled back, "I can handle the horses on my own. You go on and do what you need to." A minute later, he drove the horses from the pen. Hoofbeats disappeared down the gulch.

Grumbling to himself, Hawker dropped the reins to his horse, flipped up the stirrup, and adjusted the cinch for his saddle. Ruby held her breath. *Don't look down. Don't look down. Don't look down.*

Maude's bellering grew louder. This time Ruby recognized it as her mad-as-a-moosequatch bawl. "You old nag." Hawker stomped over to the pen. He jerked at Maude's lead, then Ruby heard a loud snap. "That'll teach you."

Ruby stared with horror. She had to do something or Maude would be gone forever. Reaching up from where she lay, Ruby grabbed a handful of branches, pulled them down, and shook them under the belly of Hawker's horse. The gray spooked. It neighed and turned, trotting away down the gulch.

"Hey!" Hawker dashed after his startled horse. The instant he passed, Ruby scrambled up. She raced toward Maude and worked furiously to untie the rope that joined her with the other donkeys. Then, just as fast, she worked the knot that secured Maude to the gate of the makeshift pen.

Maude twisted around to nuzzle Ruby then she stiffened and snorted. Ruby heard hoofbeats and a prickle shot up her spine. Ruby turned and stared into the glossy eyes of the gray horse. As she lifted her gaze, the long shiny cylinder of Hawker's gun gaped back at her.

Hawker rolled his thumb over the hammer of his gun. "You've just solved my problem." He grinned menacingly.

Hawker dismounted. He holstered his gun and grabbed Ruby by the arm. He tied her wrists with his neck scarf and threw her roughly onto Maude's back.

Hawker laughed. "You'd better keep this donkey under control." He pulled out his gun again and waved it. "Or else ..."

Ruby watched Hawker climb onto his horse. Making an effort to keep the shaking out of her voice, Ruby spoke to Maude soothingly and began to sing Maude's favorite song, "Sweet Rosie O'Grady." She changed the words to the way Maude liked them.

Sweet Maudie O'Grady,
With a cute little nose,
She's my steady lady,
Most ev'ryone knows.

After a minute or two, Maude settled into an easy walking rhythm. Ruby relaxed a little, but she continued to sing. As she did, her mind worked furiously on a plan for escape. They climbed out of Long Hungry Gulch and started east. Ruby tried to put a map in her head. They were crossing Signal Hill not too far from Lizzy's pa's claim.

Ruby wiggled her wrists, trying to loosen the bandana. Maybe she could get Hawker to stop somehow and untie her wrists. "I need a drink of water," she complained.

Hawker turned around and sneered. "You won't be needing water where you're going."

Where was that? Ruby wiggled her wrists again, but the knot seemed to tighten.

"My pa's going to be out looking for us," Ruby said. *Please Pa.* Ruby wished she'd talked things over with him first. Pa knew how to think things through, and he might have had a better plan.

Signal Hill began to disappear behind them. Ruby glanced over her shoulder and thought she saw someone standing on the ridge. When she looked back again, nothing was there.

"I don't imagine anyone's going to be interested in a few missing animals with all the fire cleanup and the looting," Hawker scoffed. "Or much worried about a spoiled, unruly girl."

Spoiled and unruly! Ruby jerked so suddenly that Maude started to bray again.

"Shut that donkey up!"

Ruby squeaked out a few more lines of "Sweet Rosie O'Grady" and hugged Maude with her knees. They dipped down, rose up, and crossed the next ridge. The outskirts of Cripple Creek came into view. She was close enough to see where the fire had burned but too far away to yell for help.

Ruby heard a shrill whistle. In the distance, a puff of smoke traced the path of the Florence and Cripple Creek train as it moved along the hillside. Hawker aimed straight for the tracks. Ruby figured they'd be crossing over and heading to one of the mines up Poverty Gulch, but which one? Gold Hill and the surrounding ridges were covered not only with working mines and mills, but also with abandoned shafts and dry holes.

Ruby swallowed hard, remembering what Hawker had said about not needing water where she was going. It would take days to find her if he decided to throw her down one of those empty pits.

She decided to risk talking. "I don't think anyone's going to want to pay good money for Maude. She's an outdoor donkey."

Hawker chortled. "They all are when they start out."

Ruby tried again. "I can just take her home. I'll never tell a soul what happened."

Hawker laughed again, a chilling cackle that sent shivers through her. "You won't be able to."

A little ways farther, Hawker stopped. He dismounted and stood near Ruby. Maude's ears shot up. "We're going to circle around back of the terminal and take the road up Poverty Gulch," Hawker said. "We'll be passing by some shacks, and I want you to look and act normal."

Hawker pulled a silver dollar from his pocket. He pitched it up in the air, drew his gun, and fired. Ruby heard a clink, and the coin fell. Hawker picked it up and showed Ruby. The edge was bent where the bullet hit. Not a bull's eye, but it was close enough to convince Ruby that she didn't want to be in Hawker's path if he decided to aim her way.

"No funny business," Hawker said. He untied Ruby's wrists. "If you try to run, I'll shoot the donkey first, and then you."

Maude pawed the ground and wrinkled her lip until her long teeth showed. Ruby could see she was working herself up to a real tantrum. "And keep that donkey under control." Hawker climbed back on the gray, and they started off again.

Ruby stroked Maude's neck and whispered, "Don't worry. I'll think of something." She sang a few more lines of Maude's song, mostly to keep her own mind settled. Her thoughts ran in circles, and every circle ended back at Hawker's gun.

The song ended as they swung around behind the Midland Terminal and cut over to the Poverty Gulch road. The rutted tracks climbed past tarpaper shacks and tents where women beat rugs and hung laundry on ropes. Children played, and men walked up and down the gulch road, carrying dinner pails and tools. No one noticed anything unusual.

Maude's ears swiveled nonstop. She was jumpy and twitchy—probably hungry and thirsty. Ruby wasn't sure how long they'd been riding, but it was long enough for her stomach to feel like a bobcat was inside prowling around. And long enough for the sun to make long shadows as it dropped down in the western sky.

Ruby shifted and glanced around, trying to pick out some of the landmarks. Pa had pointed out some of the biggest mines—the Rose, the Molly Kathleen, the Eldorado, the Gold King.

If only Pa were here. A wave of hopelessness washed over Ruby as she thought about the last couple of weeks. She and Pa had been like two grumpy bears bumping around in the same den. And all because of Miss Sternum.

Miss Sternum. Ruby's throat throbbed as she tried to swallow. She was truly sorry she'd never given Miss Sternum a chance. Now, Ruby thought, if she could get out of this trouble—and if Pa decided to marry Miss Sternum—she would make the best of it.

Ruby imagined a life of elocution class, fancy shoes, and teas, and then amended her thought. At least she would *try* to make the best of it.

Ruby forced herself back to the present. They'd left the shacks of the gulch behind and were on a long section of road below the Gold King Mine. Ruby watched a man approach. He rode a mule and wore a black hat pulled down over his face to shade it from the sun.

A short distance farther, Hawker stopped and dismounted. He removed his gun from the holster and held it to his lips, blowing across the tip. He leered at Ruby. "You've been very cooperative," he said, "so far."

The man on the mule stopped next to Hawker and nodded. "I see you brought the stock." He surveyed the string of donkeys. "Looks like they're in good condition. That front one is nice and fleshy."

Ruby stiffened and Maude did the same, backing up and tugging at the lead rope.

"She's the best one of the group," Hawker said. "She'll make a fine worker." He smiled at Ruby.

"Who's the girl?"

"She's got an affection for her donkey," Hawker said with sarcasm in his voice. "I told her she could come along with me to say good-bye."

The man shrugged. "Makes me no difference as long as I get these critters up to the mine."

"This donkey isn't any good," Ruby blurted. "She's stubborn, and she has tantrums, and ..." Hawker silenced her with a menacing look.

The mule man chuckled. "She'll get along just fine. These miners treat their work animals like pets. I wager she'll be eating right out of their hands in a couple of days."

Ruby's heart sank. It was probably true. She thought about how quickly Maude had taken to the children at school when they brought her snacks. The man handed Hawker some folded bills, and Hawker handed him the lead rope for the donkeys. *I've got to do something.* Ruby's mind raced. In a minute, Maude would be led away, never to see a sunrise or a sunset again.

"Time to say good-bye." Hawker walked back and yanked Ruby off Maude. He stood her on the ground, keeping a firm grip on her upper arm.

Ruby screamed. "No!" She shook free of Hawker and lunged for the lead rope. It slipped through her fingers as Hawker grabbed her roughly and pulled her back. She tried to wriggle free and hollered, "This man's a thief. All these donkeys are stolen. You can't have them!"

Nineteen

Hawker squeezed Ruby's arm a little tighter but spoke in a calm, soothing way, loud enough so the donkey wrangler could hear him. "I know you're upset about losing your pet, but I paid your pa fair and square so he'd have enough money for his gambling debts." He smiled up at the mule man. "I thought I was doing her a favor letting her come." He shrugged. "I guess she's as cantankerous as her donkey."

The wrangler adjusted the lead rope and shifted uncomfortably. "It's none of my business. You got your money, and I got the job of delivering these up to the Gold King."

The man reined his mule around and started up the road, towing the donkeys behind him. Maude started to bray, pulling backward on the lead. Ruby struggled, trying to wrench free of Jake Hawker's grip. He growled, "I've just about had enough of you."

Ruby twisted around and kicked at his shins. She wailed, trying to swing at him with her free arm. Maude brayed more loudly. The donkey wrangler cursed and pulled on the rope. In the confusion, the other donkeys began bawling and tugging every which way on the lines. With a final yank, the mule man succeeded in getting the donkeys lined out and moving. They continued up the road, a chorus of unhappy, out-of-step animals.

"Maude!" Ruby called after her. The bellowing continued with Maude's deafening cry echoing above the others. Again Ruby tried to squirm free, but this time, the cold steel of Hawker's gun stopped her.

"I should have dumped you in one of those abandoned mines earlier." Hawker jabbed the revolver deeper into Ruby's ribs. "And it's still not too late."

"I think it is." A voice behind them spoke.

Ruby held her breath, too afraid to hope. It was her Pa. It *had* to be Pa.

Hawker turned around with Ruby, still holding the gun to her side. He stared at the man holding a rifle. "I think you need to get on out of here and mind your own business," Hawker said.

"This *is* my business." Pa moved the butt of his rifle enough so his deputy's badge could be seen. "And if you so much as harm a single hair on my little girl's head, I'm going to use this gun for something besides hunting."

A flicker of recognition passed over Hawker's face. He jabbed the gun harder into Ruby's ribs and sneered. "You think that deputy badge is going to stop me from finishing what I started out to do?"

Pa and Hawker stood, unmoving, staring icily at each other.

"Ruby!" A loud cry came from the road below. Panting and huffing, Lizzy rushed up to join Pa. Her words gushed out. "I found him. I found your pa and brung him. I saw that man take you. I saw everything. And my pa, he's coming, too. He's plenty fired up about Mr. Hawker. We saw the donkeys pass over Signal Hill, and after that I told him about what happened and how you went down Long Hungry Gulch, and ..."

She took a breath. "My pa told me to run and get help because he didn't trust Mr. Hawker farther than he could throw him, and even though I don't reckon Pa could throw him very far, he had a pretty good idea where Hawker was heading because he was talking about the Gold King Mine when he visited Pa at his claim, and ..."

Ruby looked beyond Lizzy. Joe McAvery staggered

up the hill, half walking, half running. Behind him, Miss Sternum pedaled on her two-wheeler. As she passed Lizzy's pa, her bicycle wobbled in the dirt and fell sideways. From there, Miss Sternum lit out on foot, bustling up the road, and struggling for air as she joined the small group.

After a moment, Miss Sternum straightened up and spoke, using her strictest schoolteacher voice. "What do you have to say for yourself?"

Ruby braced for the reprimand. She was sure that Miss Sternum was speaking to her. Instead, Miss Sternum looked fiercely at Jake Hawker.

Ruby felt Hawker's arm go slack. He eased his grip on her arm and dropped his gun. Ruby lunged for it and scrambled over to stand next to Pa. She gripped the pistol with both hands and pointed it at Hawker, trying to keep her aim steady.

Miss Sternum marched over and stood nose to nose with Hawker, pressing a finger into his chest. "You ought to be ashamed of yourself."

Hawker mumbled under his breath. "I wish I'd never met any of you people. Shoulda left Cripple Creek a long time ago."

"I suppose you're not the only one that feels that way." Pa flipped a pair of handcuffs from his belt. He snapped them around Hawker's wrists.

The last to arrive, Joe McAvery shook his fist and roared, "You double-crossing, no-good thief!"

He pushed past Ruby and snatched the papers from inside Hawker's jacket. "You won't hear the end of me until you sign my claim back."

"I've got some money right now," Hawker said weakly. "I'd planned to pay you for it."

"You planned nothing of the sort." McAvery squeezed the papers and shook them at Hawker. "You were going to sell those critters and skip out on all of us. Now you sign these back over to me."

"Allow me to assist." Miss Sternum opened her purse and found her fountain pen.

Joe McAvery took the pen and the papers and held them under Jake Hawker's nose. "Get busy signing," he said.

Jake held up his handcuffs and smirked.

Pa sighed. He unlocked one cuff, keeping a tight hold of the chain with his free hand. Hawker scowled and scribbled on the papers. He started to hand the pen back, but then, with a sudden, swift move, he shoved Pa. Pa stumbled backward into Ruby. She dropped Hawker's gun, and it fired as it struck the ground. In the moment it took for everyone to realize what had happened, Hawker sprinted for his horse.

"He's getting away!" Ruby dashed after him, lunging for Hawker's leg as the horse stampeded— bucking, kicking, and snorting.

Pa reached Hawker next, pinning him on the ground. Hawker flailed and lashed out, cursing and spitting dirt. Pa yanked Hawker to his feet and jerked his arms behind him, locking the cuffs around his wrists.

Hawker snarled and snapped. "You can't do this to me. I'm a law-abiding citizen." Hawker's cheeks flamed with anger as he fought against the cuffs.

Law abiding! Ruby's own anger blazed as she thought about all the trouble Hawker had caused them—the stolen candleholders—stranding them in Cripple Creek—stealing Maude. Ruby shuddered to think what else Hawker would have done.

Pa picked up Hawker's gun and pointed it at him. He nodded toward his rifle, and Joe grabbed it. Hawker growled. "The next time I cross paths with this girl or her donkey, I'm going to …"

"Maude!" The blood drained from Ruby's face. Without wasting another second, she spun and ran frantically up the gulch, following the trail of the mule man and the stolen donkeys.

"Ruby!" Pa called after her. She might as well have been deaf. Ruby could only think of one thing: rescuing Maude.

Twenty

The roof of the shaft house for the Gold King Mine jutted into the horizon about a quarter of a mile away. Three towers stood behind it, belching black smoke. The donkey tracks led directly to the headframe for the bucket that raised and lowered men and equipment into the mine.

Breathing hard, Ruby ran past the signs that read, "Danger. Keep out!" Directly ahead, the donkey wrangler shouted orders to the crew around him. He held Maude's lead rope. "Get this last one ready." Gears squealed, and the steam hoist hissed. A huge iron bucket appeared, and the cables of the hoist stopped.

Three large men pulled Maude onto her side and tied her feet with rope. Maude twisted and snorted as they lifted her into the bucket bottom first and turned her on her side.

"Maude!" Ruby raced forward.

The wrangler blocked Ruby's way. She pushed past him, but he grabbed her by the collar and jerked her back. "Where do you think you're going?"

"I'm getting my donkey!" Ruby wiggled free. She dashed for the bucket, grabbed onto the cables, and swung over the lip just as it began to lower into the shaft.

Everything went dark. All Ruby heard was the squeal of the hoist and shouts from above. Then Maude wuffled to her. Ruby scrunched down and curled around Maude's round belly. She stroked Maude's neck. "Whatever happens, I'm not leaving you again."

The machinery moaned, and the bucket jolted to a halt. It swung eerily from side to side, clanking against the rock on the sides of the shaft. Ruby looked up at the small patch of light at the top of the lift. Everything else, inside the bucket and beyond, was as black as the inside of a coffin.

Ruby's heart pounded, and she felt Maude's chest rise and fall as the cables creaked. She imagined the whispers of the Tommy Knockers. *You'll never essssscape. Once in the mines, you can never leave, never leave, never leave ...*

Ruby snuggled closer to Maude and pinched her eyes closed; counting each time the bucket tapped the rock. *If I'm going to die, at least I'll have Maude at my side.* Something moist touched Ruby's cheek. It was Maude's rubbery lips, nibbling her face with a donkey kiss.

As suddenly as it had stopped, the grinding and squealing began again. Slowly the bucket began to rise, scraping and bumping the sides of the shaft. The light from above blinked and flickered until it flooded in and filled the metal carrier.

Ruby heard voices. Someone hollered, "Stay back!" The next thing she saw was Pa. He lifted her over the lip of the carrier. The three men who had loaded Maude tipped the bucket and dragged her out, untying the ropes around her feet.

"I thought I'd never see you again." Ruby threw her arms around Pa's middle.

Maude wobbled a little, then hopped a few steps, trying out her legs. She nosed Ruby and sniffed at Pa.

A disgruntled man with a waxed mustache said, "I guess we'd better send word down to the tunnels and get the rest of those donkeys back up here and returned to town."

"We already sent word to the sheriff," another man said.

Ruby hugged Pa again and took hold of Maude's lead. On the way back down from the mine, she told him the whole story. "I think Hawker planned to throw me down a dry hole and leave me there to eat rats." Maude snorted as if agreeing with her about Hawker's plans.

As the threesome approached, Hawker looked like a different man. He hung his head like a schoolboy who'd just had a whuppin'. It didn't take Ruby long to figure out why. Joe McAvery held Hawker at rifle point while Miss Sternum marched back and forth waving Hawker's gun like an accusing finger. "Furthermore," she declared. "If you don't change your ways, you'll end up in a place worse than jail."

It appeared that Joe McAvery was feeling the effects of the lecture as well. He flinched and ducked as if the words were meant for him. As soon as he saw Pa, he handed over the rifle and called Lizzy over. "We'd best git goin'."

Lizzy gave Maude a hug and then started down the road with her pa. Miss Sternum called after them. "I hope this will act as a reminder to you that drinking never leads to any good."

Joe McAvery sank into his jacket like a turtle trying to hide in its shell. As he approached Miss Sternum's bicycle, he made a wide swing around it and quickened his pace. Lizzy trotted after him.

"Good heavens, who could that be?" Miss Sternum pointed Hawker's gun down the road, past where her bicycle lay.

Ruby squinted. The sun was setting, making it difficult to see in the fading light. Finally she recognized Mr. Penn. When he saw Miss Sternum, he walked briskly toward her. "My dear Miss Sternum, are you all right?"

Miss Sternum stared at the gun she held as if realizing for the first time she'd been waving a weapon. "Oh my." She handed the gun to Pa and said to him, "I'm afraid I failed to mention ..." Her face turned the color of fresh beets, and she appeared to be at a loss for words. "I was on my way to cancel our evening engagement when ..." Miss Sternum turned from Pa, and looked at Mr. Penn and then at Jake Hawker, Ruby, and Maude.

Pa tucked the gun into his belt, still keeping the rifle trained on Hawker. He started to speak when Mr. Penn moved closer to Miss Sternum and said, "I was quite worried. People in town saw you head this way. Poverty Gulch is a rough place."

Miss Sternum straightened up. "Yes, quite so." She pushed her glasses up on her nose and smoothed down her bicycling skirt. She spoke crisply to Ruby. "Young lady, I shall expect you on your best behavior when you return to school after this ... this episode."

Miss Sternum glanced again at Hawker, shaking her head as if she'd just awakened from a bad dream. She hooked her arm through Mr. Penn's elbow and started down the road. As they stopped to pick up the bicycle, a man on a white horse passed them.

Even in the growing darkness, Ruby could make out the sheriff's star on his jacket. He approached and tipped his hat at Pa. "I hear there's some trouble up here."

After the story was told, Pa handed the sheriff Hawker's gun. The sheriff dropped it in his saddlebag and pulled out his own, pointing it at Hawker. "You might as well start tracking to town." He turned to Pa. "I imagine you've earned the night off."

Hawker scowled at Pa, then his eyes shifted left and right as if looking, one last time, for a way to escape. His gaze rested on Ruby and Maude, and he glared angrily at them.

Ruby wrapped her arms around Maude's neck and squeezed tightly. She watched the sheriff and Hawker disappear into the twilight. Not far ahead would be Miss Sternum and Mr. Penn. Ruby whispered in Maude's ear, "I'm pretty sure it's just the three of us again. You. Me. And Pa."

Feeling a little guilty about being so happy, Ruby glanced over at Pa. Usually she could read him like a book, but right now the pages were as blank as if a flood had rolled through and washed all his emotions away.

"Pa?" Ruby led Maude closer to Pa. The lights of Cripple Creek flickered on, one at a time, reminding Ruby of stars. "Me and Maude could sure use a drink of water."

Pa hugged Ruby. "I know just the place." The three of them detoured from the Poverty Gulch road and followed a deer trail down into a gully where a small spring bubbled up. Ruby let Maude drink first, then cupped her hands and filled them over and over again, until she thought she would burst.

Ruby sat down on a rock next to Pa. She wanted to ask him a hundred questions, like when would they be leaving Cripple Creek? Were they settled here for good? Or, now that Miss Sternum seemed interested in Mr. Penn, would he start looking to find her a different mother?

"Pa?"

"Shhhhh!" Pa held a finger to his lips. "I think I see a moosequatch."

Maude's ears stiffened, and she snorted softly. Barely visible on the ridge across from them, a large animal moved slowly in the dark. Ruby held her breath as the glow from the moon worked its way down the ridge to the place where the animal stood. It was Hawker's horse, still saddled, with the reins dragging as it shuffled slowly across the hill.

"Do you think we oughta go get it?" Ruby asked, half-hoping she and Pa could have a moonlight adventure together.

"It's too far away," Pa said, "and we're on foot." He tugged on Ruby's braid. "Besides, I've got beans cooking on the campfire."

Ruby knew Pa meant the stove back at the cabin. She sighed and grabbed Maude's lead. The three of them walked the moonlit path back toward Poverty Gulch. Maude nibbled at Ruby's shoulder, and for just a little while, the world seemed right.

Author's Note

During its heyday, Cripple Creek had its share of drinkers, gamblers, scoundrels, and thieves. However, the majority of the people were hardworking men and women who came to seek their fortunes and make a living by prospecting, mining, or working in the many businesses that a gold mining town needed for support. There were liveries, lumberyards, pharmacies, restaurants, saloons, groceries, and dry goods stores of all types and sizes. Along with this came the need for entertainment in the form of concerts and theater performances. In addition, many family activities and picnics were sponsored by social groups such as the Knights of Pythias, Order of the Eastern Star, Odd Fellows, and a variety of women's clubs.

Many people made a good living in Cripple Creek from gold mining and other businesses. But many more, like Lizzy's father, scraped by and eventually left with nothing more than the holes in their pockets to show for it. If you worked in Cripple Creek in 1896, you might expect to earn from $15.00 to $20.00 a week for clerical work, from $3.00 to $5.00 a day for mining or working as a mechanic, about $5.00 a day driving a team and wagon, and $1.50 to $2.50 a day for common labor.

Lodging was difficult to find. Renting a room might cost from $10.00 to $50.00 a month or even higher. Some of these dwellings were known as "telephone" shanties because it was said the walls were so thin you could hear the person in the next room thinking. Often as many as twenty people were in line waiting for a place to live.

People arrived in Cripple Creek on foot, in wagons, by stagecoach, or by train. Shelf Road was built in 1892 and connected Cañon City and the Arkansas Valley to Cripple Creek. Stage robberies and holdups along the road were not uncommon. Once the bandits had attacked, they could slip away easily and hide in the rocks of the canyon walls. In 1894 the narrow gauge Florence and Cripple Creek Railroad arrived, and in 1895 the Midland Terminal line was completed. This line connected Cripple Creek to Colorado Springs and areas to the north.

There were two fires in Cripple Creek during April 1896. The first one, written about in this book, was on April 25 and happened very much in the way described. One exception is that the National Hotel was not blown up as a firebreak. Its construction continued, and it eventually became the finest hotel in Cripple Creek. It was five stories high with its own electric light plant and steam-operated elevators as well as the Turkish bath and barbershop mentioned in this story. There were 40 suites and 125 rooms, but the room number 13 was eliminated. Well-to-do people, such as Cripple Creek's first millionaire, Winfield Scott Stratton, kept suites there.

During the fire, however, buildings *were* dynamited in an attempt to keep the fire from spreading. Many of the worst injuries from the fire resulted from these explosions, and it is not believed that these firebreaks did much to stop the spread of flames. Firefighters and volunteers battled to save bank safes, U.S. mail, telegraph lines, and newspapers. Men passing buckets of water to the roof of the Midland Terminal saved the building, which was scheduled for completion at the end of the month. As in the fictional story, men were deputized to control looting and keep saloons closed. Badges for the one hundred deputies were ordered and hastily cut from tin cans by a local tinsmith.

Nearly three thousand people lost their homes in the first fire and were provided shelter by the rest of the community. Of the churches in town, only the Catholic Church and the Methodist Church remained. Three other churches on the same block as the Methodist Church burned to the ground.

After the fire, rebuilding began immediately. Many businesses relocated in temporary buildings and were open for business on Monday morning following the fire, only to burn down two days later when a second fire struck.

After May 1, 1896, the town council stopped people in the fire district from building temporary or permanent wood structures. Instead, everything needed to be constructed with brick. In 1897, Cripple Creek officially became a city. Some say the updated telephone and electric systems and improved water and sewage helped to make this possible. At its peak, Cripple Creek had more than thirty-five thousand people.

Acknowledgments

Thanks to Jan Collins of the Cripple Creek Museum for answering questions about schools and social groups as well as for pointing me to other Cripple Creek resources. Thanks, also, to enthusiastic readers Shanna Lewis and Brett Mach and to my husband, Steve, for his ongoing support. Additionally, thanks to Mary Peace Finley for her astute "writer's eyes," attention to detail, and helpful mentoring. Last but not least, thanks to Doris Baker of Filter Press for promoting literature related to Colorado's history, a love we share.